THE HOR[...]

Stampede! The dread [...] jessie's mind. But it did not numb her muscles. Or her will to save herself from the oncoming horde of cattle.

She whipped her horse with the reins, urging it to move faster, willing it to *fly*. The bay sped forward, its head bobbing and its ears erect, as it splashed through puddles and over unstable ground that threatened to bog it.

Behind her, Jessie could hear the clatter and clash of horns striking one another. A harsh symphony straight out of hell.

Jessie spotted a large grove of trees standing like leafy sentinels ahead of her on the left. If she could reach the trees in time, she would have a chance of avoiding being trampled to death beneath the hooves of the oncoming cattle.

The bay beneath her began to slow. She tried to flog it into another spurt of speed but couldn't. The animal's breath was coming in ragged spurts now.

The grove was only fifty yards ahead of her now. A few moments later, only forty yards. Then, thirty.

Her horse stumbled and broke stride. She felt it going before it actually went down. Then the animal pitched forward. . . .

WESLEY ELLIS

LONE STAR

AND THE
RAILROAD KILLERS

J S

J

JOVE BOOKS, NEW YORK

LONE STAR AND THE RAILROAD KILLERS

A Jove Book/published by arrangement with
the author

PRINTING HISTORY
Jove edition/July 1990

ISBN: 0-515-10353-5

Jove Books are published by The Berkley Publishing Group,
200 Madison Avenue, New York, New York 10016.
The name "JOVE" and the "J" logo are trademarks belonging
to Jove Publications, Inc.

PRINTED IN THE UNITED STATES OF AMERICA

10 9 8 7 6 5 4 3 2 1

Chapter 1

Sights: undulating fields displaying their lush produce—golden wheat, tangled vines heavy with melons, green trees bearing a rich bounty of ripening lemons, apricots, apples, and peaches. A blue sky, empty of clouds, above it all. A faint gray haze on the distant hilltops. The gaudy flash of sunlight on the snappy brass trim decorating the engine pulling the five-car train. Sparks flying up from the engine's stack to flit past the windows like fireflies.

Sounds: the shriek of the whistle as the engine rounded a bend. The rhythmic clatter of wheels on rails, iron pounding iron. The boisterous voice of the conductor loudly announcing, "Next stop, Groveland. You will have time to eat at Groveland, ladies and gentlemen. Next stop . . ."

Smells: acrid cigar smoke. Dusty air. A woman's too-liberally applied lemon verbena.

Jessie Starbuck was aware of them all—the sights, sounds, and smells that were a part of her journey aboard the Southern Pacific train being pulled by a 4–4–0 engine, which combined impressive speed and immense power

1

as it traveled its transcontinental route toward its final destination, San Francisco.

Jessie Starbuck, daughter of the late Alex Starbuck, was, as her father had been in his time, a powerful financier and empire builder. Hers was the ultimate responsibility for the success—the profitability—of the many business interests that came under the huge Starbuck Enterprises umbrella. These business interests ranged from the buying and selling of real estate in the United States and in almost every other country of the civilized world through diamond mines in South Africa and the silk trade in the Far East to rubber plantations in South America.

She managed them all and she managed them well. Starbuck Enterprises, under her father's former guidance and now under hers, had become and remained the world's most successful conglomerate.

Jessie was as beautiful as she was successful in business. She was a woman who would turn the head of almost any man. She was tall and slender but not so slender that she lacked the attributes of ripe femininity. Her breasts were full but not ponderous. Her hips were lush and sensuous. Her waist—almost nonexistent. A man with large hands could easily span it. Her legs were lean and lithe. Her hair, which was the color of copper, framed a classically beautiful face—lean nose, full lips, prominent cheekbones, brilliant green eyes.

She was wearing a silk blouse and a brown skirt beneath her linen duster, which, though worn to keep her free of the dirt and grime that was an inevitable part of a train journey, had failed to do so. She wore black shoes on her feet and a hat that was trimmed with an ostrich plume.

Beside her sat her devoted companion, the half-Japanese and half-American, Ki. Years earlier Ki, son of an American father and a Japanese mother, had been taken on by Jessie's father, and, though hired originally as a bodyguard for Jessie, had become much more to her. He had become a valued and trusted friend.

Ki was taller than most Eurasians, part of the legacy

he had inherited from his father. His body was both compact and muscular. He wore his hair, which was black and straight, longer than was the current fashion among American men. His eyes had an Oriental cast, and they bore clear witness to the Japanese blood that flowed in his veins.

Like Jessie, he wore a linen duster over his three-piece suit. Resting beneath his hands on his lap was a brown derby.

"Well, it won't be too much longer," he said as the train began making its way through California's San Joaquin Valley.

"It will be good to see San Francisco again," Jessie said, leaning back in her seat as she continued to gaze out the open window. "I love that city. I think it's my favorite city in the whole world."

"Oh, really?" Ki gave her a sidelong glance. "When we were in Paris last year, you said, as I clearly recall, that you thought *Paris* was the most beautiful city in the world. And when our ship docked in New York and we were on our way to our hotel, you said the same thing about *that* city."

"You have a very good memory," Jessie said, an expression of mild chagrin on her lovely face. "I wish you didn't. I can't stand being caught in inconsistencies."

"Of what real value is consistency? If we were all rigidly consistent, what a dull world this would be. I *applaud* your inconsistencies, Jessie, truly I do. They add spice to a person's life. As to consistency, one must seriously consider what Ralph Waldo Emerson had to say in one of his essays. 'A foolish consistency is the hobgoblin of little minds' and so on."

"Saved by Emerson by way of my good friend and occasional mentor, Ki. By the way, I've arranged with Ben Harrison to have dinner with him this evening. You'll join us, won't you?"

"I will, although, as I recall, the chairman of the Southern Pacific's board of directors is not the most scintillating of men."

3

"What do you mean?"

"Well, when you first introduced him to me some time ago, I had the distinct impression that Harrison eats, drinks, and sleeps the Southern Pacific. That's all he talked about. What he kept calling 'his' railroad.''

Jessie laughed lightly. "I suppose you're right. Ben is rather obsessed with the railroad and its interests. He puts them above just about everything else in life. As a result, he has helped to create one of the most successful railroads in the country.''

"To give the devil his due.''

"Ben Harrison is no devil, Ki. He's a rather courtly old gentlemen, as a matter of fact.''

"I suppose a woman would see him differently. To me, he's a man with a mission, and such men make me uneasy.''

"If you'd really rather not dine with us this evening—''

Ki put out a hand and gently touched Jessie's arm. "I didn't mean to make a mountain out of a molehill. I should learn to keep my personal opinions to myself. I'll make a bargain with you. If I put up with your 'courtly' Mr. Harrison at dinner tonight while he regales us with talk of mergers and unit costs and the like, I want you to agree that I needn't attend tomorrow's stockholders' meeting. I'd much rather make the rounds of the town. Take advantage of what San Francisco has to offer while I can. Who knows when I'll get back there.''

"I don't mind at all. The meeting will be strictly business and not a great deal of pleasure—certainly not for you, it won't be. I confess I rather enjoy it, though.''

"You would. If you didn't enjoy such things as shareholders' meetings, you wouldn't be the successful entrepreneur that you are.''

"True. Still, I will confess—but you must promise to keep this a secret strictly *entre nous*—they can be boring, such meetings. One frequently finds oneself confronted by all manner of difficult, not to say eccentric, individuals. Last year, I recall, there was this cantankerous little old lady—gray hair, sturdy black shoes, metal-rimmed

4

spectacles—who quite loudly and emphatically insisted the Southern Pacific should immediately undertake to build north to the Yukon Territory because she had heard that the area was a veritable hotbed of potential profit since the recent discovery of gold there.''

"What did you tell her?"

"I didn't have to tell her anything, thank goodness. Ben Harrison told her—I'll never forget his gracious manner and mellifluous voice as he said, 'My dear madam, a most interesting suggestion, for which we thank you, and we assure you it will be given the consideration it so richly deserves.'

"Well, the woman was quite satisfied with Ben's answer. She didn't seem at all aware of the titters that ran through the audience as a result both of her bizarre suggestion and Ben's indirect and rather devious way of telling her that the board would not give the matter a moment's serious thought—'the consideration it so richly deserves.''"

Ki chuckled and then, turning serious, asked, "Has the Southern Pacific had a good year?"

"Yes, it has, I'm happy to be able to say. We've increased the amount of freight we carry by thirty-six percent this past year. Our expenses have been reduced by a rather astonishing eleven percent. I say 'astonishing' in light of the steady and burdensome increase in the cost of both materials and labor. That decrease in expenses has been a prime factor in allowing us to pay our stockholders a dividend that has increased markedly again this year."

"A clear tribute to the management skills of all of you who serve on the railroad's board of directors."

"The Southern Pacific's success has also, I'm pleased to say, contributed substantially to the overall profitability this year of Starbuck Enterprises. As a holder of almost forty percent of the railroad's outstanding shares, I've been able to bolster our overall rate of growth and expect that trend to continue in the foreseeable future."

"Stocks, bonds, debentures—when you get off on those subjects, Jessie, you lose me."

"I know, I know. You are more interested in—"

"I'll say it for you. Wine, women, and song."

"I was going to say the smell of roses, the tranquility that comes from peace of mind, the beauty of a lovely summer day such as this one."

"Those things, too," Ki said with a self-mocking grin.

They were silent for some time as the world whipped by outside the speeding train, each of them alone with his thoughts.

Ki noticed that Jessie shifted position in her seat several times. She folded her hands in her lap and then crossed her arms across her chest. She looked out the window, then across the aisle, then over her shoulder.

"What's wrong?" he asked her.

"Nothing. It's just that I'm impatient to get where we're going. This trip, for some reason, seems to be taking forever."

"Calm down. Take it easy,"

"I'm too restless for that."

"Focus," Ki said simply.

Jessie knew what he meant. He had taught her the *aikido* technique he had learned long ago in Japan for reaching an inner peace combined with a calm strength. She recalled the first time he had told her about it and then how he had taught her to apply the technique in her own life.

She had been under great emotional stress following the death of her father. She couldn't eat, couldn't sleep. She was aware of Ki watching her closely in the days following the funeral, his gaze sympathetic, his attempts to console her, however, unavailing. Her fault, she afterward realized. But not at the time. She was short-tempered. Even truculent. She felt as if she were falling apart inside and that there was no one and nothing that could assuage the pain that was tearing her to pieces as easily as if it had been a lion attacking her.

"One day in Japan," Ki said to her when this had been happening to her for nearly a week, "I saw an advertisement for an *aikido* lecture."

She turned and started to leave the room they were in.

6

Ki stepped in front of her, preventing her from escaping. "I had been interested in learning *aikido*, 'the gentle art,' for some time. I went to the lecture, which was held in a small store that had been coverted into a martial arts practice hall—a *dojo*, which means 'the place of enlightenment.'"

"Ki, forgive me, but I'm not interested—"

His steady gaze, the warmth in his almond eyes, silenced her.

He continued, "I sat down cross-legged on a practice mat with the others in the *dojo*, and soon a young Japanese man entered the room. He was wearing the black *hekama*, or skirt, of the *aikido* master. I recall that he looked vulnerable, even fragile, as he proceeded to face nearly a dozen big men who circled him menacingly.

"I winced as they all attacked him at the same time. Then I sat there amazed as he seemed to flow like water into that mass of attacking men. He moved like a fish in that dangerous sea of men, his *hekama* swirling about his legs. Every time one of the men tried to strike him, he seemed to vanish before the blow could reach him.

"The faster he moved, the calmer he seemed to be as he diverted the energy of his attackers and vanquished them all, one by one. It ended soon after it had begun. The master, still calm, bowed to the audience as they applauded his prowess. Then he bowed to his student attackers, who returned the courtesy."

"Ki, I don't see what this has to do with me."

"I later learned from the master himself, who admitted me to his *dojo* as a student, that his power was based on his expert control of his life force, his *ki*, that all martial artists, especially *aikidoists*, train to develop. The center of this *ki* is the *tai-ten*, or 'one point' located about an inch and a half below one's navel. By concentrating on the *tai-ten*, one can muster the energy of one's powerful life force and use it to defeat an enemy or to control one's own thoughts and emotions, which are, unfortunately for all of us, our inner enemies at times."

Jessie remembered protesting at the time that she was no martial artist as was Ki and that therefore such an

7

exercise would do her no good. But he had been adamant, insisting that she could indeed benefit by learning the *aikido* technique of controlling one's *ki*. Sceptically, she had followed his instructions. Doubtfully, she had practiced the methods he had taught her.

She found, in time, that her emotional distress lessened, and with it went the severe emotional pain she had been suffering.

"Have you forgotten how to control your life force?" Ki asked, his question lifting Jessie out of the past she had been recalling and depositing her squarely in the present once again.

"No," she answered.

" 'Flow with whatever may happen and let your mind be free: Stay centered by accepting whatever you are doing. This is the ultimate,' " he intoned. And added, "A quotation from Chuang-tzu, a very wise man."

Jessie closed her eyes. Focused her mind. Summoned her life force, her *ki*, let it slowly flood her body and mind. A sweet feeling of serenity gradually descended on her. Her muscles relaxed. Her thoughts stopped racing. She felt at one and at peace with the universe.

By the time the train pulled into the depot in the town of Groveland in the San Joaquin Valley, she was calm and in complete control of herself, her impatience gone, her restlessness conquered.

"Groveland!" the conductor loudly announced. "A rest and relaxation spot, ladies and gentlemen. We will sound the whistle in ten minutes when the train is due to depart. *Groveland, Groveland!*"

"Are you hungry?" Ki asked Jessie, who admitted that she was.

"We can get something to eat at the lunch counter in the depot."

Together they left the train and, ducking cinders and soot falling from the train's stack, headed for the depot at the end of the platform.

Before they reached it, Ki noticed the buxom blonde standing near the entrance to the freight office, an anxious expression on her face.

8

"You go ahead," he told Jessie. "I'll join you in a minute or two."

She glanced at him and then at the woman he was staring at. Making no comment, she continued on her way alone.

Ki's eyes roamed up and down the blond woman's lush body. Now, that's a woman born to comfort a man, he found himself thinking. Look at those lush hips and those big breasts she's got. She'd be softer than a goose-down comforter to lie upon.

The woman's blond hair seemed to glow in the sunlight, and her blue eyes were like two inviting cobalt lakes. The skin of her face was rosy and smooth, without a blemish on it anywhere.

Ki felt himself stiffening as desire surged within him. But there wasn't time. They would no doubt be at the depot no more than the ten minutes railroads customarily allowed for refreshment stops. He imagined his arms around her, imagined himself buried within her as she bucked and he erupted . . .

He looked down the platform. Jessie had disappeared. He told himself he wasn't hungry, although his stomach was grumbling. He made his way over to where the woman was standing. "Nice day," he said when he reached her and tipped his hat. "Hot, though."

She looked at him and then back at the men unloading freight from the train.

"Summer is my favorite season of the year," Ki commented, moving closer to the woman, who seemed oblivious to him. "The living's easy in summer. Not like in winter, when the wind blows and the snow flies."

She said nothing. Didn't nod. Or even look his way.

"Are you just naturally beautiful or do you have to work at it?"

His remark brought a reaction—a blush. Progress. "I'll bet you're waiting for a package to arrive."

"Yes, I am. How did you know?"

"By the way you can't seem to take your eyes off those men unloading the freight car. I also know you're

9

worried about it not being there with the other goods they're unloading.''

"Yes, I am, as a matter of fact. But how—''

"I know because of the frown on your face and the way you keep biting your lower lip. Is it an important package you're expecting?''

"Oh, yes. It's woodworks. My brother ordered them from Chicago. They're for the farmhouse he built. He bought some fret brackets and some spandrels and some corbels. Also some fleur-de-lis trim. What some people call 'gingerbread.' He's finished the house with the single exception of the decoration.''

"Miss Simmons!'' called out the freight agent, who was holding a sheaf of papers and a pencil in his hands as he scanned the crowd gathered on the platform.

"Oh, there you are, Helen!'' he exclaimed when he spotted the woman to whom Ki had been talking as she hurried toward him. "Just sign here, Helen.''

She took the pencil and form he handed her and signed on the spot he indicated. "Which one is it, Hiram?''

"That crate right there,'' was the reply.

"Oh, my. Such an enormous crate!''

"You brought your wagon to haul it in, didn't you?'' Hiram asked.

"Yes, it's down at the end of the platform. But how will I ever get that heavy crate from here to the wagon and then *into* the wagon?''

"I'd lend you a hand, Helen, but I've got to sign out all that freight piled up there. If you'll wait till I'm done, I'll help you, how's that?''

"No need to wait, Miss Simmons,'' Ki said as he joined her. "I'll load the crate on your wagon for you.''

"Why, that's very kind of you, sir. Can I help?''

"Not necessary.'' Ki bent down and lifted the crate, which turned out to be surprisingly heavy, and started for the end of the platform.

"Not that way, sir,'' Helen called out to him. "The other way.''

He turned and headed in the opposite direction, Helen Simmons hurrying along by his side.

"It's that wagon right there," she said, pointing. She let down the tailgate, and Ki loaded the package on the wagon, glad to be relieved of its nearly knee-buckling weight.

"Thank you, sir. You've been most helpful—and kind."

"You live in Groveland, Miss Simmons?"

She shook her head. "My brother and I live on a farm three miles west of town. He's not at home today or he would have come for the woodworks."

The train whistle blew three times in rapid succession.

"I've got to go," Ki told Helen. "I wish I didn't. But I'm a passenger on that train that's bound for San Francisco, and it appears that it's time to leave, although for the life of me it doesn't seem like ten minutes have gone by since we got here. But then, time flies when one is enjoying oneself as I have been enjoying myself while talking to you, Miss Simmons."

"Thank you, sir. It was a pleasure meeting you."

"I regret that we shall probably not meet again."

" 'Ships that pass in the night, and speak each other in passing; Only a signal shown and a distant voice in the darkness; So on the ocean of life we pass and speak to one another, Only a look and a voice . . . ' " Helen's words trailed away. Then, "That's by Longfellow. I think those are such sad words."

The train whistle sounded again.

Ki touched the brim of his derby to Helen and then turned and went sprinting down the platform, almost colliding with the train's conductor, who was about to enter a side door of the depot. Ki shouldered his way through the mob of people streaming out of the depot's restaurant and boarding the train in obedience to the whistle's shrill command.

Where was Jessie?

Ki found her inside the depot arguing with one of the aproned waiters behind the long counter that was littered with uneaten food left behind by the train's passengers.

"Jessie," he called out to her. "Come on, the train's ready to leave."

She paid no attention to him. "I demand that you return my money," she angrily told the counterman with whom she was arguing.

Ki went to her side and touched her arm. "Jessie—"

"The lady's right," declared an equally angry man standing on the far side of Jessie. "You make us pay fifty cents in advance before we can even place our orders, and then what do you do? You dawdle about serving us the food we order, and then, when you finally do deign to serve us, the train whistle blows and you tell us we are not allowed to take the food with us but must consume it here!"

"We *can't* consume it here!" Jessie said, her voice rising. "Not unless we want to miss the train, which I, for one, do not want to do. Sir, I insist that you return the fifty cents I paid you."

"Jessie," Ki tried again, "the train—"

"This is highway robbery!" she cried, ignoring him. "I will not stand for it."

"Lady," said the counterman in a bored tone of voice, "you can stand for it or sit for it or do whatever you want whichever way you want to do it, but them's the house rules. I already *told* you that."

Jessie's fingers formed fists at her sides.

Ki was almost certain she was going to haul off and hit the counterman. He took her firmly by the arm and marched her out of the depot.

"Let me go," Jessie demanded, shaking herself free of Ki.

He waited for her to board the train and then climbed up behind her. By the time they were back in their seats, Jessie seemed ready to explode with frustration and the fury that followed in its hot wake.

"The railroad has to keep to schedule," he told her in an attempt to soothe her. "You know that."

"I know that only five minutes elapsed from the time this train arrived here until its whistle sounded to announce its impending departure. The normal time for a refreshment stop is *ten* minutes."

12

"I know . . ."

"You heard that passenger—that man in the depot. They didn't—I swear they *wouldn't*—serve us promptly and efficiently in that restaurant. The result was what you saw. All of us lost the money we were required to pay in advance, and those few of us fortunate enough to have been served had no time to eat what we had ordered before the whistle blew."

"I know—"

Jessie stood up and announced, "I'm going to register a complaint." She stalked down the aisle and into the next coach.

She returned a few minutes later, declaring, "I can't find the conductor."

Ki recalled his last sight of the conductor. "I saw him on the platform just before I joined you in the restaurant. He was on his way into it by a side door. Where are you going?"

"To find him."

Ki followed Jessie as she left the train and made her way around to the side door of the restaurant. She went through it without a moment's hesitation with him right behind her. They found themselves in the restaurant's steamy kitchen.

Jessie stopped in her tracks as the conductor, standing with his back to her and talking to the counterman she had argued with earlier, said, "Don't you try to tell me I don't know what I'm talking about, dammit! There were fifty-five passengers on my train and forty-three of them went into your restaurant. So you owe me four dollars and thirty cents."

"I told you I kept careful count," the counterman almost shouted. "Maybe forty-three people came in the restaurant, but only thirty-four ordered food and paid fifty cents in advance for it. So your cut of ten cents per head comes to three-forty, not four-thirty."

"So that's it!" an incensed Jessie declared, striding purposefully up to the two men. "Now I know why we didn't get the full ten minutes for a refreshment stop.

13

You took our money, but you didn't fill most of our orders. What did you intend—"

"Get out of here, lady!" the counterman roared, gesturing wildly at Jessie. "Nobody but employees of the restaurant is allowed in the kitchen. *Get out!*"

"What did you intend to do with the food that was served but not eaten?" Jessie asked him, ignoring the angry order he had given her.

As he reached out to seize her, Ki stepped between him and Jessie.

"Answer the lady's question," he said in a low voice, his eyes boring into those of the counterman.

The man stepped back, seeming to wilt under Ki's intense stare. He glanced at the conductor, at Jessie, then back at Ki, who prompted, "We're waiting for your answer." And then added, "But I, for one, won't wait much longer." He raised his hands as if he were about to reach for the man cringing before him.

"Easy, mister, just take it easy now. I'll answer your question."

"Get back on board, you two," the conductor said, withdrawing a watch from his vest pocket and squinting at it. "The train's leaving in thirty seconds."

"No, it's not," Jessie said. "It's not leaving until I hear what this man has to say in answer to my question."

"We take the food that's not eaten by the passengers," the counterman said, "and we serve it to other customers."

"I see," Jessie said speculatively. "The conductor connives with you to cut the refreshment stop short. You delay serving most of the passengers who have all paid you fifty cents in advance when they ordered. Those you do serve—you keep the food they couldn't consume to serve to others."

"From the sound of things," Ki said, "you split your take with the conductor, who's in on the scheme with you. He gets ten percent of your take. That's right, isn't it?"

The aproned man, obviously frightened, could not speak. But he could nod, and he did.

14

"My name is Jessie Starbuck," Jessie said. "You'll have reason to remember my name. I happen to be a member of the board of directors of the Southern Pacific railroad, and I am telling you"—she addressed the conductor—"that I will see to it that you will be summarily dismissed from your job when we get to San Francisco, and you"—she turned to the man Ki was still facing—"will lose the right to serve passengers on the Southern Pacific. I will see to it that a new refreshment stop is chosen from among the many towns in this area."

"No," the man moaned, his eyes widening.

"Yes," Jessie said. "Now give me the money you collected from the train passengers. I intend to return it to those you attempted to cheat." Jessie held out her hand.

Ki sat alone as the train, having resumed its journey, picked up steam. He stared out the window, not really seeing what he was looking at, his thoughts drifting, the fingers of his right hand caressing one of the potentially deadly *shuriken* in his pocket.

The sharp iron blades of the five-pointed throwing star stirred his memories of what he had learned about the use of the weapon of the ninja, those so-called "shadow warriors" of feudal Japan.

Shuriken. Weapon of stealth. Silent. Deadly. Easily concealed.

Ki's index finger played over the small round pintle hole in the center of the *shuriken* he was touching. The hole, to a casual observer, might have been viewed as mere decoration. But it was far more than that. Ki had once used the *shuriken*'s pintle hole to remove nails from a locked door in order to gain admittance to a building.

His reverie was interrupted by the arrival of Jessie, who took her seat next to him.

"Everything all settled?" he asked her.

"Yes. I returned the money the passengers paid for the food they never got to eat, much to the chagrin of that shyster who calls himself a conductor."

"Ah, the remarkable ingenuity of man," Ki said. "If

15

but one-tenth of the energy and intelligence that men use to concoct and execute their corrupt schemes and scams were to be applied instead to the doing of good deeds, the world would become a veritable garden of delights in virtually no time at all.''

"Don't look for such an earthly paradise any time soon," Jessie cautioned. "Not with individuals like our conductor on the loose.''

"And his confederate, the restaurant's counterman.''

"Those dogs have had their day, to alter the old saying a bit.''

"You're going to do what you threatened?''

"I am. The conductor will be dismissed. The train will stop elsewhere for refreshments in the future. We owe it to the company's passengers. I'll let Ben Harrison handle things through proper channels once we get to San Francisco.''

They arrived at their destination that afternoon. The train depot was packed with people, those arriving and those greeting the new arrivals.

"I'll get our luggage," Ki said and left Jessie to stand staring at the vast bay sparkling brilliantly in the sunshine. She couldn't help marveling at how much the city had changed since her last visit. Market Street was busier than ever and buildings had been built on the low bluffs above it. The hills rising from the bay were almost completely covered with buildings now where once goats and sheep had roamed.

San Francisco. City born of gold and kept alive by the staunch pillars of prosperous societies anywhere in the world: industry, enterprise, and commerce.

"Jessie!''

She turned to find Ki beckoning to her. She joined him and together they made their way to the carriage he had engaged to take them to the Parker House, where they had a reservation.

When they arrived at the hotel on Portsmouth Square, Jessie was greeted by name by the doorman who opened the door of their carriage.

16

"Hello, Ralph," she said as he helped her down from the carriage. "It's nice to see you again."

"It's far more than just nice to see *you* again, Miss Starbuck," Ralph said. "We've missed you. You've stayed away much too long."

"I promise not to do it again, Ralph."

"I shall hold you to that promise, never fear, Miss Starbuck," Ralph declared with mock sternness as he finished removing the luggage from the carriage and followed Jessie inside the hotel.

Ki paid the carriage driver, and then he, too, entered the lobby of the Parker House. He was about to head for the desk where Jessie was talking to the clerk behind it when a young woman who was lounging in a leather armchair with her lithe legs crossed captured his attention. She was smoking a cigarette in defiance of accepted societal conventions, and when she saw Ki, she blew smoke in his direction as if it were some sort of insubstantial signal.

She was a slender woman, more angular than curved. There was a restlessness in her eyes and the way the fingers of her free hand tapped the arm of her chair. She didn't blink as she stared at him. She did pat her ringleted raven hair and purse her lips in what Ki thought was a decidedly erotic gesture.

She's on the job early, he thought as their eyes met and held. She apparently works hotels instead of the streets.

He started toward her, intending to express an interest in what she obviously had for sale—or, at least, for rent—when Jessie intercepted him and handed him a key.

"We're on the third floor," she told him. "I'm in room three-oh-five and your room number is three-twelve. The bellhop is on his way up with our luggage. Shall we go?"

"Room three-twelve," Ki said more loudly than necessary to make sure the seated woman with the arousing lips heard him. Then he followed Jessie to the hydraulic elevator at the rear of the lobby, which took them to the third floor.

17

Ki had barely closed the door of his room behind him when there was a knock upon it. A soft series of taps that were the very soul of discretion.

He opened the door, and there she was as he had expected.

"Please come in."

"Who is she?" the woman asked. "She can't be your wife, or you'd be sharing a room with her."

"She's a good friend. But you didn't come up here to talk about her, did you?"

"No, I didn't."

"My name's Ki."

"You can call me Opal."

"How much, Opal?"

"Depends on what you want and for how long you want it."

Ki told her and they agreed upon a price, after which Opal unbuttoned his trousers and freed his stiff shaft, which she took in her hand. It sprouted beyond her hand's confines as it throbbed and pulsed in its fleshy prison. She covered it completely with her other hand.

Ki threw back his head, closed his eyes, and moaned as she then proceeded to run her hands—her ten flickering fingers—up and down his body, touching him here, touching him there—his nipples, his navel, his testicles, his sensitive inner thighs, his buttocks.

Then, suddenly, nothing. He opened his eyes, and for an instant he thought she had gone. But she was not gone. She was on her knees before him. Looking down, he watched his rock-hard erection slip, inch by slow inch, between her lips and deep within her mouth until her lips were pressed up against his pubic hair.

She paused a moment, holding him inside her mouth while her fingers glided up and down his legs and sent chills coursing through him. Then she began to suck.

It began with a rising heat that Ki found pleasant. The heat soon became fiery. It threatened to consume him in flames of ecstasy.

The world went away. Reality, all of it that mattered, was Ki, centered now in his loins, which seemed about

18

to burst with pleasure. He thrust himself into Opal's mouth, and she took him eagerly, her tongue laving the underside of his shaft as her lips tightened on him and her head bobbed back and forth.

She made wet sucking sounds as he placed his hands behind her head and interlocked his fingers. Holding her head steady, he moved wildly, feeling himself drawing close to a climax. He moaned again as her hand embraced his testicles and then began caressing them.

He exploded with a series of grunts and groans as he flooded her mouth.

She maintained her oral grip on him until he was drained, and then she released him and rose. "Good?" she asked, wiping her mouth with the back of her hand.

"Marvelous," he said with a sigh. "You were wonderful, Helen."

She cocked an eyebrow at him and then sauntered toward the door. When she reached it, she turned and said, "Do you mind if I ask you a question?"

"No, go ahead, ask."

"Who's Helen?"

She didn't wait for his answer. As the door closed behind her, Ki asked himself the same question she had just asked him. *Who's Helen?*

Then he remembered. Helen Simmons. The buxom blond woman he had met and helped at the depot in the town of Groveland. Evidently, part of his mind had been thinking of her while Opal was so professionally servicing him, a fact he found not altogether surprising.

Chapter 2

"Good evening, Ben," Jessie said as she opened the door of her hotel room in response to Benjamin Harrison's knock. "How nice to see you again," she added, offering him her hand, which he took and, bending low, kissed.

Harrison was a tall imposing figure of a man immaculately attired in a hand-tailored gray suit. His black eyes were set deep in his skull beneath a craggy brow. They seemed to impale whatever or whomever he was looking at. His forehead was deeply lined. There were crow's-feet at the corners of both eyes and two deep lines engraved in the flesh of his face which ran from his nostrils to just below his lower lip. His skin was pallid in direct contrast to his piercing eyes. Mutton-chop gray whiskers hid his sunken cheeks and square chin. He was sixty-three but looked younger.

"I'm not too early, am I, Jessie? I must confess I was so eager to see you that I set out a bit early and was fortunate enough to be able to find a carriage almost at once."

"You're not a minute too early, Ben," she laughingly told the chairman of the board of the Southern Pacific Railroad as she ushered him into the room and closed the door behind him. "You're just like your trains, Ben. On time and well-maintained."

Harrison blushed.

"You're looking good, Ben. You've lost weight, haven't you?"

"Twenty-three pounds," replied Harrison proudly as Jessie sat down and waved him into a chair opposite her. "I've been on a strict diet for months, and Jessie, I can tell you it's been a trial and a torment to me. Salads with vinegar, no oil. Lean meat broiled—but only once a week. Fruits. Nuts. No candy. No pastries. I don't know how I have survived my self-imposed regimen. But tonight is going to be different, I promise you—and myself. For weeks now I have been barely subsisting on foods I loathe, but I have promised myself that I shall throw caution to the winds tonight and dine luxuriously with you, my dear. Yes, luxuriously. We'll go to the Occidental Restaurant. It's the very best in town. Do you know it? Of course you do. We went there together when you were last in San Francisco, did we not?"

"Yes, Ben, we did, and as I recall the evening, it was most pleasant. I'm sure tonight will be the same."

"Tell me, how have you been?"

"Fine, Ben, just fine. Busy as usual, but that is nothing new for me. I seem to thrive on action."

"You have been thriving, I can see that. You're lovelier than ever, my dear. Simply radiant, if I may say so."

"You may indeed say so. I have a quite vulgar weakness for compliments."

"You deserve them. Why, if you had lived in an earlier time and Paris had seen you, he would not have looked twice at the lovely Helen of Troy."

"You remember Ki, don't you, Ben?"

"Ki? Ah, yes, your Oriental friend and devoted companion. I do remember him. He is well?"

"Yes. I asked him if he would like to dine with us

22

tonight, and he welcomed the invitation. He's looking forward to meeting you once again.''

Harrison, stroking his whiskers, said, ''I am disappointed, my dear, sorely disappointed.''

''What's wrong, Ben?''

''I had hoped you and I would have a quiet little tête-à-tête tonight. During it I had hoped to be able to persuade you to chuck everything and run away with me to sail the China Sea amid clouds of jasmine perfume under a beautiful amber moon. But now you tell me I am to have a rival for your affections.''

''Ben, you romantic roué, you know you have no rival for my affections. What other merely mortal man could hope to match your charm, your wit, your rugged good looks?''

''Another of your many lovely attributes, Jessie. You are kind to over-the-hill old men like me who have fallen under the spell of your beauty and grace.''

''Shall we go?''

''I have a carriage waiting.'' Harrison rose and took the short black cape Jessie removed from the back of her chair. He helped her put it on over her emerald dress, which had three yellow silk panels set in its full skirt. Then he escorted her to the door, where he bowed her out of the room in a fashion that was at once both gallant and reverent.

Jessie led him to Ki's door, on which she knocked.

It was opened a moment later by Ki, who was attired in a black suit, white shirt, and purple cravat.

''Good evening, Mr. Harrison.''

''You're ready, I see,'' Jessie said to Ki as the two men shook hands.

''I've been looking forward to our dinner engagement ever since Jessie told me that she had arranged for us to dine with you tonight,'' Ki said.

''This night will be the calm before the storm,'' Harrison sighed as the trio made their way downstairs. ''Tomorrow is an entirely different story. More like something from Tennyson's 'The Charge of the Light Brigade.' ''

Quoting from the poem he had referred to, Harrison intoned,

> " 'Into the jaws of Death,
> Into the mouth of hell
> Rode the six hundred.' "

"Southern Pacific stockholders' meetings are bad, are they?" Ki asked as they made their way through the lobby and out into the street.

"Madness, my good man. Sheer madness is what they are. But they must be endured."

"Ben thinks Southern Pacific stockholders have a personal grudge against him," Jessie said, smiling and taking the arms of the two men flanking her as they walked toward Harrison's carriage.

"They *do*, my dear. I swear to you, they truly do. They would put my neck in a noose if they had half a chance to do so. If I report a ten percent rise in profit, you can rest assured that someone in the audience will want to know why it isn't *twenty* percent."

Harrison melodramatically clapped a hand to his forehead, causing Jessie to smile, and then he helped her into the carriage. He and Ki joined her, and the carriage pulled away, moving swiftly through San Francisco's gas-lit night, the carriage horse's hooves clattering on the cobblestones.

They found the Occidental Restaurant crowded, as always, when they arrived some time later. The dining room sparkled with cut glass and gleaming silver, not to mention the precious jewels many of the female patrons were wearing. They were shown to a table near a window by an obsequious maître d'hotel who knew Harrison, to whom he had the sommelier present the establishment's wine list.

Harrison consulted with Jessie and Ki concerning their choices from the elaborate menus they had all been given by a waiter, and when their decisions were made, Harrison ordered a white Bordeaux from the Médoc district of France.

24

When the wine steward and waiter had gone, Harrison leaned forward and, with a conspiratorial wink at Ki, said, "I envy you, sir."

"You do?"

"To be the constant companion of such a lovely young woman—a fate very much to be desired, I say."

"It is not an unpleasant one."

"Not an unpleasant one, he says. My word, surely that is the understatement of all time!"

"If you press the point, Ben," Jessie said, "all my secrets will be revealed."

She looked down at the raw bluepoint oysters that had been placed before her as Harrison exclaimed, "What are her secrets, Ki? Such a wonderful woman must have many. It is so, yes?"

"My unbridled temper," Jessie said sweetly, and ate an oyster. "My willfulness. My occasional sulkiness."

"Her more than occasional bullheadedness," Ki added before forking an oyster into his mouth.

"Am I then to understand that my idol has feet of clay?" Harrison asked playfully, and Ki answered as playfully, "Feet and, I sometimes think, also a head of clay."

Jessie almost choked on the oyster she was swallowing.

Harrison's laughter boomed.

Jessie couldn't help smiling at Ki.

"Jessie," Harrison said, "even with feet of clay, is a far more glorious idol than others with feet of *gold*."

The frivolity ended following the second course of green turtle soup when Jessie said, "We had an interesting little experience on the way here, Ben, that I think you ought to know about."

They were finishing the main course—goose with applesauce for Jessie, stuffed roast quail for Ki, wild turkey with grape jelly for Harrison—when Jessie concluded her account of the scheme engineered by the Southern Pacific's conductor and the counterman at the depot restaurant in Groveland.

"I'll not have such scoundrel's shenanigans on my

25

railroad!" Harrison declared angrily. "That conductor will be dismissed immediately. We will arrange for another town to serve as the refreshment stop instead of the one in Groveland that attempted to cheat our passengers—and would have were it not for your intervention, Jessie."

"Which one?" Ki asked. "We saw a number of nice little towns along the way."

"I can't at the moment tell you that, Ki," Harrison replied, taking a sip of his wine. "We won't just reach out and arbitrarily choose another town. No, there is a better way. We will have a sort of auction."

"Auction?" Jessie prompted. "I don't follow you, Ben."

"To have the right to be a refreshment stop on my railroad," Harrison said, "a town must be willing to pay. Let me hasten to point out that such a franchise is a privilege. The franchise will be the prize, and we will ask the towns in the area to bid on it. The town that offers us the most service, the best food, and the highest monthly fee for the privilege will be awarded the franchise."

"That's an interesting way of going about things," Jessie mused as the waiter cleared the table. "I'm not sure I would have seen the awarding of a refreshment stop franchise as a potential source of additional revenue for the railroad."

A smiling Harrison reached out and patted Jessie's hand. "Let a wily old man give you some sound advice, my dear. Everything that comes up in a daily running of a business must be viewed as a potential opportunity to increase cash flow—*everything*."

"It might be wise to check all the restaurants that offer refreshments for sale along the Southern Pacific line," Jessie suggested. "This may turn out not to have been an isolated incident but part of a network of such schemes."

"You are perfectly right, my dear," Harrison said, withdrawing his hand. "May I suggest that you report on your ugly experience in Groveland at our meeting

26

tomorrow? It will be an opportunity to elicit any information about such scandalous practices elsewhere that may be known to our far-from-too-shy-to-speak-up stockholders."

"I don't want to interfere with your planned agenda, Ben. Perhaps you had better mention the matter when you address the meeting."

"Your deference is both polite and respectful, my dear, but, no. You experienced the scheme first-hand. You can tell our stockholders about it far more colorfully than I ever could. Besides which, they will be pleased—especially our male stockholders, who are in the majority—to hear from an attractive woman such as yourself instead of from a ready-to-be-put-out-to-pasture codger such as myself."

"You're no more ready to be put out to pasture, Ben, than I am to be put in my grave," Jessie said firmly. "A seasoned war-horse like you has more battles to fight down the road."

"Battles to fight and wars to win," Harrison said somewhat smugly as the waiter placed servings of charlotte russe in front of him and the others at the table.

"I suppose," he said as he began to eat his dessert and the waiter poured coffee for him, "that you two think me overly involved in my railroad."

Neither Jessie nor Ki said anything.

"Well, when it comes right down to it, I suppose such an accusation would have to be considered an accurate one. I *am* involved in my railroad and have been since I first joined the company as a tracklayer. Over the years, as I rose to my present position within the company, I came to identify closely with the Southern Pacific. Its interests became my interests. If it was hurt, I suffered, too. Its friends became my friends; its enemies mine."

"You've obviously been a dedicated employee of the company," Ki said, watching Harrison closely for a reaction to his use of the word *employee*.

"Dedicated, yes," Harrison said, finishing his dessert and lighting a cigar. "An employee, not quite. I've been something more to the Southern Pacific than a mere em-

27

ployee. And it has been more than a mere collection of reports and investments and the like to me. I have been to it a devoted and faithful lover, if that's not too florid a way to put the matter. My railroad has been to me down through the years a loving if sometimes harsh mistress who demands her due, which I am and have always been willing to give her.''

"You make me feel faintly guilty, Ben," Jessie said softly. "I must confess that I have nowhere near the devotion to the company that you so obviously have.''

"There is absolutely no reason for you to feel guilty, my dear. I am quite aware that my relationship with my railroad might be considered too intense by some and by other less sensitive souls as even laughable. So do not feel guilty. Your cooler concern for the well-being of the company is undoubtedly not only to be desired but to be preferred to my passion. For you it is simply one more business to be given proper attention but not your heart and soul.''

Jessie, feeling faintly uncomfortable in light of the turn the conversation had taken and in the face of Harrison's fiery-eyed intensity when he spoke of "his" railroad, glanced at Ki, and he, knowing his friend well and reading the message that was in her eyes, said, "A most delicious dinner, Mr. Harrison, don't you agree?"

"What? Delicious? Oh, yes, of course." Harrison leaned back in his chair, his breathing rapid but gradually beginning to slow.

"I really hate to end this rendezvous," Jessie said, grateful to Ki for having guided the conversation into calmer waters. "But we have a long day ahead of us, Ben, and I for one could use a bit of beauty sleep.''

"I shan't detain you a moment longer, then," Harrison said and summoned the waiter.

Ki reached for the check the waiter was presenting, but Harrison shook his head and proceeded to pay it.

They said their good-nights some forty minutes later after Jessie and Ki had stepped down from Harrison's carriage in front of the Parker House.

"Ten sharp tomorrow morning," Harrison reminded Jessie.

"Ten sharp," she repeated. "Thank you again, Ben, for a lovely evening."

"It's been a pleasure, sir," Ki said, shaking hands with Harrison.

Then, as Harrison's driver eased the carriage out into the flow of traffic, Jessie and Ki made their way into the hotel.

"To hear Harrison talk," Ki said, "was a bit like listening to a lovesick swain. I never met a man in love with a railroad before."

"Any woman would be delighted to have such a devoted consort. Few are so lucky as is the Southern Pacific vis-à-vis Benjamin Harrison. But that's all to the good, I suppose. He does no one any harm in his dedication, and he does the holders of stock in the company a great deal of good, which is, after all, his first and foremost responsibility."

"I know and you are, of course, right. I'm just glad you and he are on the same side."

"What do you mean?"

"Just this. I'd hate to see you on any side that opposes what Mr. Harrison considers the best interests of his beloved."

"By 'beloved' I take it you mean the Southern Pacific."

"That's right."

Jessie stopped at the elevator. When the doors opened, she stepped in, but Ki didn't follow her.

"You're not coming up?"

He shook his head. "I think I'll look in on what the sporting men are doing for a while, and then I'll turn in. Have a good night, Jessie. Pleasant dreams."

When the doors of the elevator closed, Ki made his way into the immense room that was filled with games and gamblers. Crystal chandeliers hung from the ceiling. The walls were paneled in oak, and the long bar on one side of the room that was being heavily patronized was an intricately carved piece of solid oak. Paintings hung on the walls—paintings of women wearing diaphanous gowns or merely frothy draperies which partially exposed their lush endowments. Brass spittoons were placed strategically on the floor bordering the oak baseboard.

Ki wandered from table to table. He watched a poker game in intense progress for several minutes. Then he spent some time watching players engaged in the French game of *vingt-et-un*. All around him men and a few women were betting their luck against the house in three-card monte, faro, or on the wheel of fortune's spin.

Ki moved on, stopping to study the paintings and to listen to a German orchestra which had just begun to play, although no one in the vast room seemed to be paying any attention to its earnest music-making.

When he came to a table where several men were shooting craps, he paused again. He watched as the play continued and bets ranged from two dollars to several hundred dollars.

One of the players bet fifty dollars, shook the dice in his hand, rolled them—and scored a natural, an eleven. The man continued playing his game of craps. On his second roll he scored a five.

"Make your point," said the gambler running the game. "Good luck to you, sir."

The player shook the dice in his hand, blew on them, and then rolled them. A nine. Next throw: an eight. The man had a thin film of sweat on his forehead as he shook the dice again and rolled a three.

"Sorry, sir," said the houseman, scooping up the dice. He rubbed them together between his palms, raised them above his head, and then swung them from side to side.

Ki found the man's movements almost mesmerizing, as did, it seemed, the other players.

The gambler made his bet, and it was matched. He threw the dice and came up with a six. He rolled them again, trying to make his point: the six. Ki watched closely as the man made his point on the very next time out and won. He continued playing and won the next two times before throwing a two and crapping out.

The man next to Ki took the dice; bets were placed and the game continued.

Ki, watching the dice, became aware of the fact that something was bothering him. He stared closely at the dice. Was he merely tired after the day's long train ride and subsequent dinner engagement so that his perceptions were faulty? He blinked. He rubbed his eyes. No, it was true. He had kept careful count. Not once since he had been watching did he see a player roll a seven. He continued watching closely. The gambler rolled a seven and won.

Suspicion continued to grow in Ki as he watched the play. He began to move around the table on the fringe of the crowd that included both players and mere spectators. Before another five minutes had gone by, he was sure he knew what was going on in what was definitely a crooked crap game. He reached out and seized the dice the gambler had been throwing.

"I say, sir!" the indignant man exclaimed. "I have not yet made my point nor have I crapped out. I think the very least you could do is have the patience, not to mention the common decency, to await your turn."

"You're not playing anymore, mister. Not with this pair of dice you're not." Ki examined them and then handed them to a man standing next to him. When the man looked blankly at the dice, Ki said, "Those are crooked. They're misnumbered. Take a close look at them. One of them has two aces, two fives, and two sixes on it. The other one's got two threes, two fours, and two fives on it. With that pair of dice it's impossible to roll a seven, though you can roll an eleven.

"It's hard to catch a sharper like this fellow because you can only see three sides of a cube at one time. Notice how the duplicate fives for example, are opposite each other, making it hard to spot this man's deception."

"This is a fair game," insisted the gambler. "Give me those dice, sir, and let's get on with the game."

The player did as the gambler asked, and the gambler then proceeded to repeat his almost mystical motions with the dice before taking bets and rolling the dice again.

Before they had even stopped rolling, Ki reached out and picked them up.

31

"Dammit, leave those bones alone!" one of the other players shouted at Ki.

"Now, this is a *fair* set of dice," Ki said. "One that's properly numbered. That gambler's been switching from this set, which he's been letting his opponents—you fellows—use, to the other one that he's rigged to stack the odds of winning in his favor. With the other one he can't roll a seven, but he can roll an eleven, like I told you. But more to the point, he can't crap out, not the way those dice are numbered, but he has a better than good chance of making his point every time he plays. Gentlemen, you have all been cheated in this game."

"There is no other set of dice," the gambler said sharply. "Do any of you gentlemen see such a mythical set that our Oriental friend here has obviously imagined? No, of course, you don't. So let us get on with our game."

"If there's a second crooked set of dice," said one of the players, "I'll be damned if I know where it's disappeared to."

Ki quickly rounded the table. As quickly, he frisked the protesting gambler and came up with the pair of crooked dice, which had been hidden in a chamois pouch sewn onto the inside of the left sleeve of the gambler's *jaquette*.

"Here's his slick trick," Ki said, displaying the hidden pouch for the spectators to see.

He had no sooner done so than the gambler lunged at him, reaching for the pair of crooked dice. Ki backed up out of the man's reach, and as the gambler drew a hideout gun from a shoulder holster and took aim at him, Ki raised his left leg and sent it flying upward in a swift snap-kick. His foot slammed into the gambler's midsection, doubling the man over.

A round plowed into the carpeted floor as the gambler's finger reflexively tightened on his gun's trigger.

Ki, maintaining his balance, delivered a second blow with the ball of his left foot, an *ago-geri* or chin-kick. It snapped the gambler's head backward, and his gun fell from his hand.

Ki gave the gambler a sharp vertical chop to the side of the head with his right hand, a blow that instantly rendered his opponent unconscious. He stepped back as the gambler crumpled to the floor.

"You've killed him!" one of the spectators breathed, looking at Ki with an expression of awe that was tinged with fear.

"He's not dead," Ki said. "He'll regain consciousness in a little while. When he does, I suggest you may not want to continue playing craps with him. Good night, gentlemen." He turned and left the room without looking back.

The sun was ablaze in the sky over San Francisco when Jessie arrived at the opera house that had been rented for the stockholders' meeting at nine-thirty the next morning. It set the bay to sparkling and softened the many sharp edges of the city in its warm yellow light.

Jessie paid the carriage driver and got out. She halted, her eyes and ears assaulted by the sight and sound of the men and women marching back and forth in front of the opera house. Some of them were carrying signs. All of them were chanting rhythmically in response to the eager urgings of a black-bearded and blue-eyed young man who seemed to be the leader of the demonstration.

The signs read: SEND THE SOUTHERN PACIFIC SOUTH TO HELL; WE WILL NOT BE RAILROADED; and DOWN WITH TRAINS—UP WITH PEOPLE.

"What do we want?" the blue-eyed man yelled, waving his arms as he exhorted the marchers circling him.

"*Our rights!*" they shouted back.

"What'll we do if we don't get them?" he bellowed.

"*Fight!*" the marchers bellowed back.

Jessie attempted to make her way through the mob of marchers but found the going difficult. She could not say for sure that the chanting men and women were deliberately blocking her path, but she was sure that they were not making her passage an easy one.

Finally she managed to get through them, resisting the urge to clap her hands over her ears to shut out the sound of their raucous chanting. She had almost reached the door of the opera house when she suddenly found her path blocked by the tall young leader of the demonstrators whose followers were now silent as they watched him and Jessie.

He stood in front of her, his arms folded across his brawny chest, his booted feet planted far apart, a look of stubborn determination on his ruggedly handsome face. His blue eyes seemed to blaze as hotly as the sun itself as he gazed down at her. From him emanated an aura of pure power, one that Jessie found intimidating and, at the same time, oddly exciting. His workman's flannel shirt seemed about to burst at the seams as it tried to contain his body. His jeans, patched in two places, seemed about to do the same as they attempted to contain his strong legs and loins.

"Please let me pass," Jessie said to him in a neutral voice, her eyes meeting his.

"Ma'am, you don't want to go in there and be a party to the truly terrible things the railroad's been doing to us ordinary folk."

"You are quite wrong. I do want very much to be a party to what the railroad is doing since I happen to be a member of its board of directors."

Her words seemed to shock the man confronting her. His blue eyes seemed to darken to black. His smooth forehead wrinkled in a frown. His nostrils flared.

"You—you must be the Jessie Starbuck we've heard talk of."

"I am. Now, if you will please step aside—"

"No, Mike Brandon does not step aside or step down or kneel or bow his head or do any of the other things that high-born and higher-placed muck-a-mucks such as yourself demand that low-born folk such as myself do in your haughty presence. It's for your own good that I'm keeping you from attending the meeting of the railroad's criminal accomplices, by which I mean its stockholders. I want to keep you from becoming a party to the Devil's own work, which is exactly what will be taking place inside come ten o'clock this morning."

"I notice that you are allowing other interested parties to enter the building," Jessie pointed out as several people made their way past her into the opera house.

"It's you I'm concerned with, Miss Starbuck. If I can convert *you* to our way of thinking—"

"You can't." Jessie attempted to step around Brandon, but he stepped in front of her, once again effectively blocking her way. She was about to pound the high heel of her shoe into his instep when a whistle shrilled.

"Police!" one of the marchers cried.

"Stand firm, lads and lasses!" another marcher called out.

Jessie turned in time to see the police, billies swinging, wade into the mob. Within seconds they had laid several men low and were dragging two women to a paddy wagon that had pulled up to the curb.

Brandon darted into the midst of the melee of flailing billies and falling bodies only to be immediately clubbed to the ground by one of the policemen, causing Jessie to wince. She watched the officer drag the unconscious Brandon to the paddy wagon and unceremoniously throw him inside.

Marchers dropped their signs as they tried to protect themselves from the policemen's clubs. Some of them fled.

Jessie stood transfixed, seemingly unable to move, until the area was cleared of marchers, the paddy wagon had driven away, and the remaining policemen had departed on foot, swinging their clubs and proudly smiling. Then she turned and went into the opera house.

She made her way down the sloping aisle and climbed up onto the stage, where several men were gathered together, Benjamin Harrison among them.

"Ah, Jessie, there you are!" he cried when he saw her. "We'll be ready to begin soon." He pulled out his watch and opened it. "In eleven minutes, to be precise."

"Ben, what was all that commotion about outside just now?"

"Commotion? Oh, you mean those demonstrators. Nothing to worry yourself about. A bunch of rabble

35

roused by a relentless troublemaker named Mike Brandon. When I arrived and saw them, I immediately sent for the police to disperse them.''

"Mr. Brandon, I gather, was the man with the blue eyes who was leading the demonstration?''

Harrison nodded. "Did he—did they—give you any trouble?''

"Nothing worth mentioning. What are their grievances against the railroad? I gather they have some, judging by the signs they were carrying and by the rather vague remarks this Mr. Brandon made to me about the Southern Pacific.''

"The people you saw are settlers on land owned by the railroad. Some of them have lived on that land for years now. They dispute the price at which we have now offered to sell them the land on which they have been homesteading.''

"Ben,'' said a man who hurried up to Harrison with a sheaf of papers in his hand. "Are these figures correct? They seem rather high to me, and I don't want to present inaccurate information to our stockholders.''

"They are correct, I assure you, Charles. We have just increased our terminal rate by eight percent.''

"We have? That is news to me. I thought we were having enough difficulties with the terminal rate as it was. It's been one of the more troublesome bones of contention between us and the public we serve. Do you think an increase at this time is warranted in light of the difficulties we've been having?''

"Jessie, say something soothing to calm our distinguished friend and fellow board member, Mr. Chalmers.''

"Hello, Charles,'' Jessie said and offered Chalmers her hand.

"Oh, Jessie, forgive me. I didn't see you standing there. I had better visit my ophthalmologist since I have trouble noticing such a beautiful woman.''

"Or your undertaker, Charles,'' Harrison said with a boisterous laugh.

"It's almost ten o'clock,'' Chalmers noted.

"I'll be right with you, Charles." Harrison offered his arm and Jessie took it. He escorted her to a seat on the stage among the other board members, and then, after running a hand over his whiskers and smoothing down his hair, he took up a position behind the lectern set in the center of the stage.

"Ladies and gentlemen," he began, addressing the seated stockholders. "We welcome you to our annual stockholders' meeting, and I know I speak for the other board members when I say we are most gratified at your continued strong interest in our company, which is attested to by your presence here this morning.

"Now, let us get down to business. I have here a copy of the Southern Pacific's annual report, as I'm sure you have as well. I would like to go over it with you, line by line and detail by detail, so that you will all have a full understanding of just what the past fiscal year has been like for your company. I begin with our cash position as of June first of this year. Our net assets at that time totaled . . ."

Jessie took from her reticule her copy of the Southern Pacific's annual report and followed Harrison's summary of the year's performance.

He went over the year quarter by quarter, skimming over the third quarter in which the railroad showed a decline in revenue and hurrying on to the year-end figures which showed an increase in profitability unequaled in any of the previous years. When he was finished some time later, he graciously introduced Charles Chalmers, the secretary of the corporation, who proceeded to read off a list of transactions involving government land grants, acquisition and retirement of rolling stock, liquidation of certain items of corporate debt, and assumption of new obligations.

Jessie looked up from her copy of the annual report. She scanned the audience. The men and women in it sat quietly, pleased looks on their faces, as they absorbed what Chalmers and then Evan Stiner, the company's president, had to tell them. Following Stiner came Dennis McManus, company treasurer, who pointed out to the

37

audience how much Southern Pacific's shares had increased in value over the past five years, a summation which was followed by enthusiastic applause from the attentive shareholders.

Harrison once again took the lectern when McManus stepped down. "I must tell you all in complete candor that our company has encountered a few problems during the past fiscal year. Revenues from our San Francisco to San Diego route have not been what we hoped they would be, indeed, fully expected them to be. But we look for a substantial increase in revenue from this route in the year to come. Likewise, we have not done as well as we thought we would . . .

Jessie waited expectantly for Harrison to refer to the demonstrators who had been so vociferous outside the opera house, but he made no mention of them or their concerns, which struck her as odd. But she had no time to give the matter much thought because Harrison was in the process of introducing her.

"We are happy to have with us this morning Miss Jessica Starbuck, chief executive officer of the world-renowned Starbuck Enterprises, who has brought to my attention a matter of some concern. Not a serious matter, ladies and gentlemen, let me hasten to assure you, but one which must not and will not be allowed to continue. It is a problem Miss Starbuck encountered on her way here to this meeting aboard one of our trains. She spoke to me about it, and I promise you I will correct the matter as expeditiously as possible. I want her to tell you what she experienced, and then, if any of you have experienced a similar problem while traveling on the company's trains, we hope you will take this opportunity to bring it to our attention so that it, too, may be resolved quickly and to our passengers' complete satisfaction. Miss Starbuck?"

Jessie rose and went to the lectern as Harrison resumed his seat. "Good morning, ladies and gentlemen. It is a distinct honor for me to be able to address you this morning about a matter that concerns us all. I was, as Mr. Harrison has just told you, on my way to San Francisco

38

aboard a Southern Pacific train when we came to a refreshment stop at Groveland, California.''

Jessie proceeded to outline the scheme that had been concocted by the train's conductor and the counterman at Groveland to defraud the passengers of the money they had paid for food.

"Now, this is a serious matter which concerns us all—"

"It doesn't concern me!" a male voice roared from the back of the auditorium. "But I'll tell you what *does* concern me and other settlers like me. The grasping greed of the railroad monopoly is what I'm talking about, and I'm here to tell you all about it and ask you to demand of your board of directors that something be done about it and done immediately."

"Who is that man?" Charles Chalmers cried, rising from his seat on the stage and pointing at the man standing in the front of the auditorium.

Jessie knew the answer to Chalmer's question. "That man" was the blue-eyed Mike Brandon who had earlier tried to prevent her from entering the opera house to attend the stockholders' meeting.

Chapter 3

"Please sit down, Mr. Brandon, and be quiet so that this meeting may continue," Jessie said sharply.

Brandon's response to her request was loud mocking laughter.

A man next to Brandon shot to his feet and, pointing at Jessie, shouted, "You have no right to tell us to sit down and be quiet! We won't be quiet. We won't sit down. Neither will we tolerate any longer what your railroad and the men who work for it are doing to us."

"Sir, I did not *tell* you to do anything. I merely *asked* you to show common courtesy so that—"

Brandon's laughter once again erupted, and then, to the man standing next to him, he said, "That's her, Bill. That dame's the famous—maybe I ought to say *in*famous—Jessie Starbuck. Miss Starbuck, I'd like you to meet Bill Fowler, who's a good friend of mine and a fellow fighter in the settlers' struggle against your railroad and its devilish way. Bill, say hello to the lady."

Fowler didn't say hello. Instead, he gave Jessie a

sweeping—and mocking—salute in the form of a deep bow from the waist.

"Chet Langley!" Harrison shouted from behind Jessie. He got to his feet and scanned the auditorium. "Where is our chief of security?"

"I'm right here, boss. At your service."

The man who had responded to Harrison's call was tall and lean. He had a weathered face and the eyes of a ferret. His words had emerged from his mouth around the plug of tobacco he was chewing.

"Remove those men!" Harrison ordered, indicating Brandon and Fowler.

Langley summoned two uniformed guards, and the trio started down the aisle from his seat at the rear of the auditorium toward the men Harrison had named.

"You can't strong-arm us out of here!" Fowler shouted at Harrison. "We've got a right to be here. This here is our right!" He held up a certificate that identified him as the owner of one share of Southern Pacific stock.

Brandon did the same.

Langley reached the men and gestured toward the rear of the auditorium.

"Ben," Jessie said, turning to Harrison, "as stockholders in the company, those men have every right to attend this meeting and to make themselves heard."

"Their rights be damned!" Harrison blustered and gestured to Langley, indicating that he was to proceed with the process of removing Brandon and Fowler from the auditorium.

"How many of you stockholders know what your company's been up to down in Fresno County?" Brandon shouted. "How many of you know that the railroad's been evicting homesteaders from the very land the railroad brought us here to settle on years ago?"

"That's just about enough out of you, Brandon," Langley snarled.

"Nice tactics, ladies and gentlemen, aren't they?" Brandon shouted sarcastically to the people in the audience, who were all watching him with rapt attention.

42

"Don't they make you proud of the way your company runs its business?" Fowler asked.

"And runs roughshod over ordinary folk like Bill and me?" Brandon added.

"Most of you didn't see the police outside," Fowler said. "You didn't see the way they clubbed us and hauled us away for disturbing the peace, as they put it. He's the one put them up to it, you can bet your boots on that." Fowler pointed an indicting finger at Harrison, who stood fuming on the stage, his hands formed into impotent fists. "But when the judge let us go, we came back. We'll keep coming back till we beat the railroad at their dirty game."

"See this, ladies and gentlemen!" Brandon bellowed, bending his head to display the bloody spot where a policemen's billy had landed. "That's the way your company's thugs treat decent hardworking people who have the guts to stand up and fight for their rights against the railroad's terminal rate and their running us off land that is rightfully ours."

"The railroad has recently taken title to the land the government granted the line!" Harrison thundered. "We gave you and all the other settlers on the land the right to buy it from us."

Brandon gave a derisive snort. "King Croesus himself would have a hard time paying the price you're asking for the land, Harrison!"

"*Langley!*"

In response to Harrison's shout Chet Langley, with the help of his guards, marched Brandon and Fowler toward the exit.

"Ben," Jessie said, "this is wrong. Those men have a right—"

The rest of her words were drowned out by Brandon's shouted words as he stood with his right fist raised at the exit to the street. "We'll stop you! Somehow we will. We'll not let you beat us down to the ground like dogs."

"We'll keep on fighting you, Harrison!" Fowler shouted.

"And we'll win in the end!" Brandon crowed. "Mark

43

me well, Harrison. We'll beat you before this thing is over and done with!''

Langley shoved Brandon and Fowler through the exit and out of the audience's sight and hearing.

Harrison joined Jessie at the lectern. ''If you're finished with your report, my dear, I'd like to say a few words about the matter raised by those two intruders upon our peaceful meeting.''

Jessie, as she took her seat, wondered how Harrison could possibly consider Mike Brandon and Bill Fowler intruders on the Southern Pacific's annual meeting when both of them were stockholders, albeit minor ones.

''First of all, ladies and gentlemen,'' Harrison began, ''let me offer you my most sincere and profound apologies for the unfortunate interruption in our proceedings. Those men—''

''What were they talking about, sir?'' an elegantly dressed man in the audience asked.

''That was what I was about to explain to you.''

''They said something about being evicted from land they own,'' the man who had just spoken said with a frown. ''I don't like the sound of that one bit.''

A murmur of agreement rippled through the audience following the man's words.

Harrison, making an obvious effort to control his growing impatience, said, ''The settlers who have been evicted did *not* own the land they were living and working on. The Southern Pacific, in its early days here in California, encouraged people, as you know, to come to this lovely state and set up housekeeping. They did and it was a mutually advantageous arrangement. They settled on portions of land granted the railroad by the federal government, and they prospered, most of them. Those who did not soon moved on to greener pastures. The railroad benefited in terms of increased passenger and freight traffic in both directions.

''Now that the company has taken title to the land involved in the government's grant, we have offered settlers the chance to buy the land from us on which they are living. I'm sorry to say that many of them, like

Messrs. Brandon and Fowler, whom you just heard speak here today, refuse to pay the fair price our appraiser has set for the land in question. The settlers apparently believe that the land is theirs. Never mind the inescapable fact that they do not have title to their land but merely reside on and use it at the railroad's sufferance.''

A woman in the audience rose to her feet. ''I think those two hotheads were making a mountain out of a molehill. You've all heard the chairman of the board, Mr. Harrison. The settlers can have the land. *If* they're willing to pay a fair price for it. If not, the company can evict them. The matter seems to me to be cut and dried.''

A smattering of applause followed the woman's remarks.

''Are there any more questions?'' Harrison asked. ''Since there are not, I propose that we adjourn for a leisurely lunch and return at two o'clock to complete the business before us. Thank you very much for your kind attention, ladies and gentlemen.''

''By the large the meeting went well,'' Jessie said to Ki that night over supper in the Parker House's restaurant. ''There were a few people who expressed dissatisfaction with the Southern Pacific's recent earnings-to-expenses ratio, but Ben explained to them that we had incurred unusually high expenses during the past fiscal year as a result of having to replace a great deal of track. Then, too, labor costs are increasing every year at what to me is an alarming rate.''

Ki nodded and finished the last of the snow peas that had been served with his rare roast beef. ''Did you bring up the Groveland matter?''

''Yes, and I had no sooner finished doing so than the fireworks started.''

''The fireworks?''

''There were two men at the meeting. Mike Brandon and Bill Fowler by name. They were part of the contingent of demonstrators outside the opera house when I arrived.''

''Demonstrators?''

Jessie explained: "It seems Brandon and Fowler were freed by the police along with the others who had been rounded up, and the two men proceeded to make their way into the stockholders' meeting. They have no love for the Southern Pacific, apparently. They accused the railroad—the members of the board, actually—of treating them unfairly in the matter of the line's land they presently occupy. Land owned by the railroad that they've been working over the years ever since the company encouraged them to come to California and settle on part of our federal land grant in Fresno County."

"It sounds to me as if they're malcontents," Ki commented when Jessie had finished telling him about what Brandon and Fowler had had to say at the stockholders' meeting. "It may be that they hope to intimidate the railroad—Ben Harrison, you, the other board members—into reducing the per-acre price for them."

"That may very well be the case." Jessie ate a piece of her succulent swordfish steak and then, pointing her fork at Ki, added, "Or it may be more than that. Mike Brandon struck me as something more than a mere conniver. He was—he seemed so—well, idealistic. He seemed sincerely dedicated to the cause he had espoused on behalf of himself and the other settlers. It's hard for me to believe that the only reason he's fighting the railroad so vigorously is to get a few dollars chopped off the sale price the railroad's appraiser has established for the land at issue."

"They may have it in mind to embarrass the company in order to get their way," Ki suggested. "I'm talking about their demonstration outside the meeting. That kind of highly visible trouble is the equivalent of hot copy to many newspapers in this country. If they could get themselves enough publicity, it might turn out that the company would quietly make them a more palatable offer to keep things from getting any worse. Companies, like Caesar's wife, must be above reproach. If they're not, they had better make sure that nobody knows about it. Especially not the press and its eager minions."

"You may be right. But if that is, indeed, what they

46

have in mind, I, for one, will not be swayed. Should a suggestion be made that the fair per-acre price be reduced, I will vote against it. I'm sure Ben Harrison will, too. In fact, I consider it highly likely that all the board members would vote against such a proposal.''

The waiter appeared and Jessie ordered coffee and apple strudel, Ki tea and vanilla ice cream.

The discussion over dessert turned to what lay ahead of them. Jessie suggested they leave San Francisco on the early morning train heading north to Oregon.

''You're still uneasy about conditions in the lumber camps,'' Ki observed.

''I am, yes. I don't know what the trouble up there is, but I know there is trouble. I can't believe that those four fires we had in the forestland Starbuck Enterprises controls were acts of God—or Nature, either, for that matter.''

''Forest fires can be started by such a simple thing as lightning,'' Ki pointed out. ''Or through careless smoking.''

''The weather was clear at the time of each of the fires. Smoking is not allowed in the forests, and the loggers obey the rule. I think those fires were deliberately set, and I intend to find out why and by whom.''

''Well, that's a problem for the future. For now, I'm not going to concern myself with the matter. What I'm going to concern myself with is seeing if I can strike it rich on the turn of a card or the spin of a wheel.''

''No gambling for me tonight,'' said Jessie. ''I'm tired. I'm going to bed.''

After leaving the restaurant and bidding each other good night, Ki headed for the hotel's casino and Jessie took the elevator to her room.

She had no sooner closed and locked the door behind her than someone knocked on it.

She unlocked and opened it and stood staring in surprise at her visitor. ''What do you want?'' she asked him.

''I want you,'' he answered.

The knock on his door caused Ki to stir in his sleep.

"It's eight o'clock, sir," a male voice called from the hall outside. "You left word at the desk that you wanted to be awakened this morning at eight o'clock. Sir?"

"Thank you," Ki called out and then lay with his face buried in his pillow, listening to the sound of footsteps receding in the hall outside his room.

Then he got up, washed, and dressed. He left his room and went to Jessie's, where he knocked softly on her door.

No answer.

He knocked again, more loudly this time. Still no answer.

"Jessie?"

No reply.

"Are you awake, Jessie?"

When he got no response, he tried the door. It swung open. Had Jessie forgotten to lock her door last night before she went to bed? Hard to believe. She was careful about such things. Especially in large cities like San Francisco, where crime ran rampant and an unlocked door was an open invitation to danger, if not outright disaster.

He entered the room, his eyes taking in the bed that had not been slept in and the shades that were up. It was possible, he reasoned, but highly unlikely, that she might have made the bed herself after getting up earlier this morning. But the maid would see to that. She might have forgotten to draw the shades for the night. Or she might have drawn them last night before retiring and then raised them before leaving the room this morning.

Unsatisfying speculation with no foundation in fact.

Had she changed her mind about going to bed last night? Had she instead decided to go out on the town? But, if she had, she surely would have returned by now, since she knew they had an early train to Oregon to catch.

Ki thought back to their parting in the lobby following dinner the previous evening. She had left him and headed for the elevator. He had seen her enter the elevator, and he had seen the doors close behind her.

He turned and left the room, closing the door behind him. Instead of waiting for the elevator, he bounded down the stairs to the lobby, which was practically deserted at this hour of the morning. He made his way to the hotel's restaurant. Jessie wasn't there among the few early risers. Nor was she in the casino, which was populated only by scrubwomen. He went to the desk and asked the clerk behind it if he had seen a young woman— he described Jessie to the man—enter or leave the hotel.

"I know Miss Starbuck, sir, and I haven't seen her this morning. Of course, I only came on duty a few minutes ago."

"Where's the night clerk?"

"Awakening guests who left wake-up calls, sir. He should be back any—ah, here he comes now."

Ki turned to see the night clerk crossing the lobby.

"Good morning, sir," the man greeted Ki as he went behind the desk and took down a coat from a wall peg.

"Before you go," Ki said, "I'd like to ask you a question."

"Sir?"

"I'm looking for a friend of mine—"

"He's looking for Miss Starbuck, Henry," the day clerk volunteered.

"Have you seen her?" Ki asked the man who was slipping into his coat.

"Yes, sir, I saw her last night when she left the hotel."

"You saw her leave the hotel last night?" a surprised Ki inquired. "What time was that?"

"A few minutes after nine o'clock."

Ki recalled having glanced at the lobby clock when they left the restaurant. The time had been sixteen minutes before nine o'clock.

"She was with a gentlemen, sir," the night clerk told Ki.

"Where did they go?"

"I really couldn't say, sir. I was rather busy at the

49

time with the day's receipts. All I can say with certainty is that they left the hotel."

"This gentleman that you saw with Miss Starbuck. What did he look like?"

The night clerk scratched his head as he tried to remember. Then, haltingly, he gave Ki a sketchy description of the man he had seen with Jessie.

"Thank you." Ki left the lobby and stood outside the hotel, barely aware of the people passing by as he considered his next move in light of the little information he had concerning Jessie.

The description of her previous night's companion that he had been given by the night clerk didn't fit anyone he knew. Could he have been one of her Southern Pacific colleagues? A member of the board of directors of the company? Had he come to Jessie on company business?

Ki doubted it, but there was one way to find out. Hoping he was not worrying unnecessarily and yet unable to explain to himself Jessie's sudden disappearance when she knew they had an early train to catch, Ki headed for the San Francisco offices of the Southern Pacific Railroad.

They were open when he got there, and he asked to see Mr. Benjamin Harrison. He was directed to an opulent office on the second floor, where he was told by a woman seated at a desk that Mr. Harrison was not in.

"When will he be in, do you have any idea?"

"Mr. Harrison usually comes in by ten o'clock but not always. Sometimes he arrives a bit later. Have you an appointment with him?"

Ki shook his head.

"I'm afraid Mr. Harrison will be very busy when he does arrive," the woman said, taking out an appointment book and opening it. "Would eleven o'clock tomorrow morning suit you?"

"No, it wouldn't. I have to see Mr. Harrison and I have to see him today. As soon as he comes in. I'll wait."

Ki took a seat, ignoring the woman's annoyance,

which had pinched her face into a sour scowl and turned her eyes to ice.

He tapped his fingers on the arm of his chair as his gaze kept returning to the banjo clock on the wall. He crossed his legs. Uncrossed them. Crossed them again.

People came into the office, bringing papers to the woman and taking away those she handed to them. Ki fidgeted. He considered leaving. . . . And doing what? Going where? He stayed where he was, and at last, at ten twenty-three, Benjamin Harrison sailed through the door of the office. He halted when he saw Ki, who was rising from his seat and heading toward him.

"Good morning, Ki. Is Jessie here with you?"

"No, she's not, Mr. Harrison, but it's Jessie I came here to speak to you about."

"Jessie?" When Ki nodded, Harrison took him by the arm and ushered him through a door on the far side of the room into an even more opulent office which was furnished with a marble-topped desk as big as a ship's deck, chairs and a sofa upholstered in red Chinese silk, and windows bordered by gold velvet drapes.

"Please sit down, Ki," Harrison directed as he took a seat in a swivel chair behind his immense desk. "Now, then. What's this about Jessie?"

"To be quite frank with you, Mr. Harrison, I don't know how to answer your question. But let me try to explain. Jessie and I had planned to leave on the first train out this morning for Oregon, where she has some business matters she wanted to look into. However, when I went to her room early this morning, its door was unlocked and she wasn't in it. I haven't been able to locate her. I spoke with the night clerk at the Parker House, and he told me he had seen her leave last night shortly before nine o'clock—with a man."

"Jessie is a very attractive woman, so it doesn't surprise me to hear that she had an engagement with a man."

"She had no engagement," Ki said. "I had left her only minutes before the night clerk said he saw her leave the hotel. She told me she was going to bed."

"Obviously she told you a white lie."

51

"I don't think so. I know Jessie too well. If she had had an engagement, I'm sure she would have mentioned it to me. She didn't. She said she was tired and was going to bed."

"But she didn't."

"Apparently not."

"What is it you want me to do, Ki?"

"I thought you might be able to tell me if one of your board members might have had reason to visit Jessie last night on business."

Harrison pursed his lips and shook his head. "That seems highly unlikely, though not improbable. Things sometimes come up unexpectedly, you know, in a business such as ours. One of the men might have run into something that led him to want to consult with Jessie. Do you know what the man in question looked like?"

"The night clerk described him to me. He said the man had blue eyes. He described him as a rather good-looking fellow."

Harrison leaned forward, his palms pressing on his desk. "Blue eyes, you say?"

"Yes, sir, that's what the night clerk told me."

"What was he wearing?"

"The man didn't say."

"It could have been Mike Brandon. Brandon has blue eyes and is considered by many to be a not unattractive fellow."

"Who is Mike Brandon?" The words were hardly out of Ki's mouth when he remembered having heard the name. He thought for a moment and then dredged up the memory of Jessie telling him at dinner about the disruption at the stockholders' meeting. The disruption that had been caused by two men, one of whom was named Mike Brandon. "I know who he is," he told Harrison. "Jessie mentioned him to me last night in connection with the disturbance at your meeting yesterday."

Harrison picked up a pencil and twirled it in his fingers. "Now, what in the world would Jessie be doing with that rabble-rouser, I wonder?"

"It may not have been Brandon. Lots of good-looking men have blue eyes. It could have been someone else."

"True, true," a thoughtful Harrison mused, his eyes on the pencil in his hand. Then, looking up at Ki, he said soberly, "I don't like the sound of this one bit."

"I don't mean to alarm you, Mr. Harrison. It's just that Jessie's unexplained disappearance—perhaps I should call it her unexpected absence—puzzles me. It is uncharacteristic of her to vanish without a trace or without leaving word for me. I suppose the best thing for me to do at this point is to return to the hotel and hope that Jessie will reappear with some perfectly sensible explanation for where she has been and why."

"I'm sorry I can't be of more help to you, Ki. May I ask you to let me know if—when—you hear from Jessie?"

"I thank you for your concern, Mr. Harrison. I'll be sure to do that."

Ki left the office and was descending the steps to the main floor when he heard Harrison call his name. He retraced his steps and found the board chairman standing in the doorway of his outer office and beckoning excitedly to him. Ki rejoined the man, and as he did so, Harrison handed him a grimy piece of paper.

"After you left, my secretary gave me that note," he said. "She said someone delivered it five minutes ago. The envelope in which it arrived was addressed to me. Read it."

Ki began to read the penciled note, feeling the muscles in his body constrict as he did so.

We have Jessie Starbuck. If you don't want anything bad to happen to her, lower the terminal rate and sell the settlers the land you own at the original agreed-upon price of two-fifty to five dollars per acre. Do it fast. If you don't or if you go to the authorities about this, the lady will die.

53

Ki looked up from the unsigned note as Harrison said, "I'll bet dollars to doughnuts Mike Brandon is behind this."

"Obviously whoever wrote this"—Ki tapped the paper with a finger—"kidnapped Jessie last night."

"That certainly appears to be the case."

"What I want to know is why."

"Obviously for the reasons stated in that note. The settlers want to buy railroad land at a bargain price, not at the price that our appraiser says it's worth. They also want the terminal rate reduced. This is the way they have apparently decided to go about having their demands met. By kidnapping one of the members of our board of directors."

"I don't know anything about terminal rates or land prices," said Ki. "I do know I want Jessie returned safe and sound. Now the question becomes how do we go about accomplishing that goal, which, I'm sure, you share with me."

"Why, of course I share it with you, Ki. To think of Jessie in the hands of those desperate men—it sends chills through me."

"Then you'll meet the settlers' demands—lower the terminal rate and reduce the price of the land the railroad has for sale."

"Come into my office."

Once inside it with the door closed, Harrison sat down behind his desk, leaned back, and steepled his fingers beneath his fleshy chin. "As I said, Ki, I am in complete sympathy with your feelings in this matter, and I, like you, want to be sure that no harm comes to Jessie. However, it must be pointed out that giving in to the demands made in that note—which, by the way, amounts to blackmail—would not be the way to achieve that end."

Ki frowned. "Do I understand you to say—"

"I am saying that the Southern Pacific cannot and should not bow to the demands of the settlers and their ringleader, Mike Brandon. If we were to give in on the two points raised in that note, there would be no end to it. After that they would want more concessions. Then

54

still more. As I say, there would be no end to it. Were we to give in to their demands now, we would be placing ourselves and the railroad in an untenable position, one that would do irreparable harm to the company, to our stockholders—"

"Mr. Harrison," Ki said tensely, "I'm sure from the sound of things that you appreciate the seriousness of this situation. Jessie has been kidnapped and the writer of that note has threatened to kill her if you do not accede to his wishes. Now you say you cannot—or will not—meet his demands. Do you realize that by taking such a position you are in effect signing Jessie's death warrant?"

"That is an entirely uncalled for accusation," Harrison blustered. "I am signing no one's death warrant. I am merely doing what I am being paid to do, which is to foster and protect the Southern Pacific's interests. I would be derelict in my duty were I to do otherwise. I'm sure Jessie, if our positions were reversed, would do the same thing."

Ki wasn't so sure about that. He forced himself to remain calm. "You said before that you think this man Mike Brandon is behind the kidnapping."

"Him and others, undoubtedly. He has a right-hand man by the name of Bill Fowler. There are many other settlers who enthusiastically support Brandon and do whatever he tells them to do. Unfortunately, they are like putty in his hands. He is a silver-tongued demon and a man capable of working other men into a frenzy. When he addresses a crowd, it soon becomes a mob."

"Where can I find this Brandon?"

"You're not thinking of going up against him and the rest of the settlers on your own, are you?" an incredulous Harrison inquired, his eyebrows rising and his eyes widening.

"Somebody's got to and I'm that somebody. We can't report the kidnapping to the police here in San Francisco or the law in Fresno County, either. You read the note. If we were to do that, whoever's got Jessie would kill her. Even if the law was brought in on this, I'd go after

55

the kidnappers on my own. I can't do nothing, not when my best friend has been kidnapped and is in danger of losing her life."

"I understand. Of course, you must take whatever action you deem necessary. As for myself, I shall speak to Chet Langley, our chief of security, and arrange for him to take appropriate measures to protect the remaining board members, as well as myself. We don't want to give Brandon a chance to choose another chicken to pluck at will."

Harrison blanched when he saw the disgusted look on Ki's face and the fire in his eyes. "I am sorry, Ki. I'm afraid I just used a most unfortunate figure of speech. Please believe me when I say that I misspoke myself. I have the highest respect for Jessie and don't want to see so much as a hair on her head harmed."

Ki fought to control his temper. He swallowed the angry words that were welling up within him and demanding to be spoken to this man who seemed to him to care more for Southern Pacific profits and the safety of himself and his colleagues than he did for Jessie. "Where does Mike Brandon hang his hat?"

"I don't know. He had a homestead near Groveland in Fresno County until we evicted him for squatting on railroad land."

"You mean you evicted him when he refused to pay the price you were demanding he hand over if he wanted to keep his land."

"Well, yes. But what we did, it was all perfectly legal. Sometimes I wish we had not run him off as we did."

Ki waited, wondering about the reason for Harrison's expression of concern for Mike Brandon. He soon found out that the concern was based on self-interest.

"If we had let him go on roosting where he was," Harrison continued, "chances are good he wouldn't have joined the settlers' fight against the railroad, and he wouldn't have become that group's fiery-tempered leader. Mike Brandon is, I feel I must warn you, Ki, a formidable opponent."

56

"A desperate one, too, if your theory about him having kidnapped Jessie and written that note to you is true."

"Oh, I've no doubt that both things are true, no doubt at all. From the description you gave me—it was Brandon who kidnapped Jessie from the Parker House."

"Where have the settlers' protests been centered?"

"Principally in Fresno County. Where are you going, Ki?"

Ki was almost at the door. He turned and answered, "I'm going to Fresno County to see if I can find and free Jessie."

"But—but you don't know that Brandon has taken her there. She could be here—right here in San Francisco."

"She could be," Ki admitted. "But I have no leads to follow here. If I go to Groveland, I just might be able to find out something that will put me on her trail—hers and Mike Brandon's."

"I urge you to be careful, Ki. Mike Brandon and the settlers he has turned against the railroad are a desperate and dangerous bunch."

"At the moment I'm feeling a bit desperate myself. I've also been known to be dangerous by one or two men I've crossed swords with in the past. I mean that last remark literally. Maybe when I locate Mike Brandon, he might find he's finally met his match."

"*If* you find him. And if you don't discover that it is you who have met your match in Mike Brandon."

★

Chapter 4

Ki was the only person to leave the Southern Pacific's San Diego-bound train late that afternoon when it stopped briefly at the Groveland depot. The platform was empty, but there was a customer seated at the counter of the depot's restaurant. Ki went inside.

The counterman, as he approached Ki, suddenly halted. "You," he said. "What do you want?"

"I'd like a cup of tea and any information you might happen to have about a man named Mike Brandon."

The customer looked up at Ki and then at the counterman.

"We don't serve either tea or information here," the counterman said. "Not to the likes of you, we don't."

"I'd always heard that Californians were noted for their friendliness to strangers. Are you fixing to prove that wrong?"

"Groveland's a friendly enough town," the counterman muttered. "But I'm not friendly. Not to you. Not after what you did to me the last time you and your lady friend was here."

I should have known, Ki thought. That fellow's got no love or even liking for me since I helped Jessie put an end to the way he was cheating the Southern Pacific's passengers.

"What about you?" Ki asked the customer sitting near him. "Do you know where I might find Mike Brandon?"

Before the man could answer, the counterman said, "This here's the Chink that got the railroad to rip the rug out from under us. Him and his lady friend got the railroad to cut me off as a refreshment stop and give the business to some other town."

"That so?" The customer glared at Ki. "Why should I tell anything to somebody who does damage to our town's economy, can you tell me that, Chinaman?"

Ki suppressed the impulse to tell the man that he was half Japanese, not Chinese. "Did your friend behind the counter happen to tell you why the railroad cut this place off as one of its refreshment stops?"

"Get the hell out of here!" the counterman yelled.

"This is a public place. I've got a right to be here."

"This says you don't." The counterman reached for a wooden potato masher, which he brandished threateningly.

"You'll clear out of Groveland if you know what's good for you, mister," said the customer Ki had questioned. "This town's got no use for railroad agents."

"I'm not an agent of the railroad."

"So you say," the customer responded, his voice dripping with scepticism. "So you say."

As the counterman, potato masher firmly in hand, moved out from behind the counter, Ki left the restaurant. Looks like I'm off on the wrong foot, he thought as he wandered aimlessly down the platform. I've not made a very good beginning. I've made a bad one, as a matter of fact.

Jessie watched her captor move about the room like a restless jungle cat. He put another log on the fire in the hearth. He went to the window and looked out. He left the window and paced back and forth on the far side of the room. He built a cigarette and lit it. Puffing on the quirly, his head wreathed in smoke, he continued pacing.

Jessie, despite her anger at him and despite her deep-seated wish to get out of this room and far away from him, could not help but notice—and admire—the sensuous grace with which he moved. Every step he took was purposeful and powerful.

When his steady gaze fell on her, she almost flinched. His eyes—they seemed to impale her. They seemed to be able to see inside her. She wondered if he knew what she was thinking. She hoped he couldn't tell what she was feeling. She had fought the intense feeling of desire for him that had swept through her as she, his prisoner, sat beside him in the carriage as he drove south from San Francisco to this place, wherever it was.

She had seen no towns during the journey. Had he deliberately avoided them? She had determined they had traveled south by tracking the path of the sun. She felt now as if she had fallen off the edge of the world and into this other world, into this small world that consisted of just one large room in a log cabin that she shared with—him. She couldn't bring herself to even think his name, let alone speak it aloud. If she spoke his name—aloud or even silently—she would, she believed, somehow lend legitimacy to her plight. It would make real the series of events that she was still trying to convince herself could not have happened, had not happened to her. But in the deepest center of her being, she knew her attempts at self-deception were failing her and failing fast.

"Dammit!"

The word he had spoken startled Jessie as if it had been a gunshot.

He dropped the quirly on the dirt floor, ground it out with the heel of his boot, and sucked on the finger he had burned while he paced, once again lost in thought.

When he glanced at Jessie, this time she neither flinched nor looked away. Instead she asked a question. "What do you hope to accomplish by kidnapping me?"

She wasn't sure he would bother to answer her since

throughout the drive south he had said very little and had chosen to ignore similar questions she had put to him at the time. But now, there was a shift in his stance, a flicker of his eyes, and a forthcoming answer to her question:

"Bring the men who run your railroad to their knees, that's what I hope to accomplish."

Jessie gave him a faintly contemptuous smile. "Surely you don't really believe that you can accomplish such an absurd goal?"

"I not only believe it, I'm banking on it the same as every other settler is who remains on the land the railroad gave him."

"You're making a desperate move, Mr. Brandon, and desperate moves seldom, if ever, succeed. They are usually made in haste, which means they are made thoughtlessly, which, in turn, means sloppily. I'd say this move of yours—kidnapping me—is not only thoughtless and sloppy but foolish as well. It won't get you what you want, whatever that may be in your twisted way of thinking."

"Twisted way of thinking? You dare to say that to me?" Mike Brandon strode across the room toward Jessie, and she drew back from him, believing that he was about to strike her. He did not. With his arm raised, he shook a finger in her face as he said, "You know nothing about what's been going on here in Fresno County."

Exultation swept over Jessie. So Mike Brandon was so clever, was he? He wasn't clever—or smart—enough to have kept her whereabouts a secret from her. Granted that she did not know precisely where she was, but now she did at least know in a general way where she was being held prisoner—in Fresno County.

"You come here once a year," an angry Brandon continued, "and you make your pretty speech to other rich people like yourself, and then everybody pats everybody else on the back about how much money they're all making, and that's the end of things as far as you're concerned for another year. Well, let me tell you something, lady."

Brandon's finger continued to shake in front of Jessie's face, almost mesmerizing her, as he continued his impassioned monologue.

"The railroad brought us out here back in the sixties by the carload, like we were cattle they were importing."

"I know they encouraged people to come here and settle. I know that they didn't charge you full fare, and I also know that they gave you incentives of various kinds to settle here, including but not limited to—"

Brandon snorted contemptuously. "Listen to the lady! She talks like a Philadelphia lawyer."

"—incentives such as free hay, free wells, plank roads, windmills—"

"Of course they gave us incentives. They did so because they had to. This area was a veritable desert at the time. What wasn't desert was a swamp. The soil was dry as dust and virtually incapable of cultivation. There was no vegetation anywhere to speak of, with the single exception of a few struggling artemisias that served mostly to provide a place for scorpions and sidewinders to get out of the scorching sun.

"It was a hardscrabble time for years for the lot of us, I can tell you. We had to build ourselves an irrigation system, and by God, we finally did build it, and we turned the desert into a Garden of Eden with barley, wheat, and fruit trees and more growing and prospering on the land."

"The Southern Pacific has offered you all the chance to buy the land you've settled on," Jessie interjected. "You can't deny that."

"I *don't* deny it. Not for one minute do I deny it. But I don't think you know half the story, Miss Starbuck. The railroad's agents gave us letters that said in part— I can quote this from memory since the words are burned on my brain— 'If the settler desires to buy, the Company gives him the first privilege of purchase at the fixed price, which in every case shall only be the value of the land, without regard to improvements. The lands are offered at various figures from two-fifty upward per acre. Most are for sale at from two-fifty to five dollars.' But now they're offering us the land at an appraised value of twenty-five to thirty-five an acre, which they call a fair price and I call highway robbery. Most homesteaders can't pay that high a price.''

"Well, I imagine that's because you homesteaders have improved the value of the land, which has resulted in a substantial increase in its price.''

Brandon turned and strode over to the window. He stood there, chuckling, until Jessie said, "Do you find me amusing, Mr. Brandon?''

"I do, Miss Starbuck. I find you most amusing. Like us, you missed the weasel words in that railroad offer that I just quoted to you.'' Brandon turned around to face Jessie, his manly figure haloed in the sunlight streaming through the window. "' '... without regard to improvements,' '' he quoted again. "Do you understand now? Do you understand that the railroad, when they gave us their original offer, stipulated that we could purchase the land at some future date at only the value of the the the land itself, not taking into account the value of any improvements we made on it.

"Which is ridiculous!'' Brandon cried, slamming a fist down on a wooden table. "What did they think we were going to do with the land? Sit on it? Or cultivate it? Ridiculous,'' he repeated but less forcefully this time.

Jessie turned the matter over in her mind. Then, "The railroad is treating you fairly, Mr. Brandon. Land in California has appreciated in value rapidly ever since the time of the Gold Rush. I think the twenty-five to thirty-five dollar per acre price represents present fair market value for the land.''

"That price takes into account the improvements we've made to the land. It takes our irrigation system into account. The homes we've built. Our outbuildings. It takes into account the wheat and barley crops growing on the land from which the growers are being evicted on a daily basis and their crops and their land turned over to speculators who come in here and buy from the railroad at what is, for them, a relatively cheap price in terms of

64

what they turn right around and sell it to somebody else for.

"What do you say to a man and his wife and to their children, all of whom have worked and slaved in the hot sun from can-see to can't-see to raise their crop, and then they have it taken—I say stolen, by God—right out from under them by agents representing your money-mad railroad backed up by the guns of railroad thugs."

"You're claiming that the Southern Pacific's agents evicted people from railroad land with the use of force?" an incredulous Jessie asked. "I don't believe it."

"It's true whether you believe it or not. Do you remember that fellow Ben Harrison called on to get rid of Bill Fowler and me during the meeting when I tried to speak my piece? I'm talking about Chet Langley."

Jessie remembered the lean Langley. She nodded.

"Him and a few like him come along with your agents when they're fixing to evict somebody. Like they did only last week to the Copelands. Amos Copeland and his wife and their four youngsters. The Copelands had a field full of wheat standing as tall and as pretty as you please when the agent Langley and his gunmen came on the scene. They had Milton Fassbinder with him. Fassbinder's a good customer of your railroad, a big shipper of fruit to Chicago and points east. Fassbinder had already paid the railroad a thousand six hundred and twenty-four dollars against a total purchase price of six thousand two hundred and eighty-eight for the Copeland homestead. Langley and the men siding him were armed with pistols, a Spencer rifle, and two shotguns.

"Amos Copeland hadn't even so much as a squirrel gun. But Langley shot him anyway when he and his wife refused to walk away from their wheat. But walk away he did, him and his wife and their kids, when Langley shot and wounded him a second time. Amos is working as a swamper in a saloon now. They broke him. You and your fat-pocketed colleagues did, Miss Starbuck! How does that make you feel?"

When Jessie made no answer, Brandon continued, "Some of us argued that we should take the railroad to

65

court. I wasn't one of them. But the majority won, so we hired ourselves a lawyer and went to the local court. We lost. The court sided with your kind."

"My kind, deep down, Mr. Brandon, is the same as your kind. We love, we hate, we fear—"

"You're rich, Miss Starbuck, you and your kind. Me and my kind's not. That's why you win and we lose. Or we did lose up until the time I brought you here. Now the wind's changing, and I can hear what it's whispering. It's saying fight for your rights, Brandon. Put one of their own in jeopardy, and you'll soon see who turns out to be top dog in the end."

"You would have been wiser to confine your efforts to win your case against the Southern Pacific to the courts and not turned to kidnapping, Mr. Brandon."

"Oh, we're sticking to the courts, too. There are those among us who believe we have a better chance in the courts than an icicle has in the halls of hell. I don't happen to agree with them. The lawyer we hired, he filed an appeal to the circuit court, which ought to be heard any day now."

"If you win your case, then you can let me go."

Brandon studied Jessie for a moment, his eyes boring into hers. "I could, yes. *If* we win our case. Which I've already told you I don't think we're about to do. So it's more than likely you'll keep simmering in the stew I've got you into until Ben Harrison and his board of directors boys decide to knuckle under to us in order to bring you back among them again."

"When will you inform Ben—Mr. Harrison—of this situation?"

"I already have. The day after you and I left San Francisco, a messenger delivered a note I wrote to Mr. Harrison."

"A note?"

"It told him we had taken you, and it told him we wanted him to lower the terminal rate and stop the evictions and to sell us our land at the original price of two-fifty to five dollars per acre right away if he wanted us to set you free."

"Ben is not a man who will sit still for blackmail, and that is exactly what you're practicing in this instance. He'll go to the police, and you and the men cooperating in this illegal act with you will find yourselves imprisoned so fast it will make your heads swim."

Brandon permitted himself a sardonic smile. "I think you're wrong about that, Miss Starbuck. Ben Harrison won't go to the law. He'll simply do what I told him to do."

"You don't know Ben Harrison."

"Maybe I don't. But I do know that I told him in the note I sent him that if he brings the law into this, you're a dead woman."

Jessie, as she digested the information Brandon had just given her, felt for the first time that she was in serious danger. For the first time since Brandon, a knife hidden in his hand, had abducted her from the Parker House in San Francisco, she considered her situation to be one that could only be described as bleak.

"Mr. Brandon, I have a proposal to make to you."

"A proposal? I merely kidnapped you, Miss Starbuck, I have no intention of marrying you."

Jessie caught the sly gleam in Brandon's eye. She saw the corners of his mouth start to curl in what might have been a smile. So the man has a sense of humor, she thought, underneath all his righteous indignation and idealistic fervor. Maybe he's human after all.

"Now I see it is your turn to be amusing, Mr. Brandon," she said. "What I had in mind actually was this. Free me. Let me return to San Francisco—"

"*No!*" The thunder of Brandon's expostulation echoed in the room.

Jessie held up a hand in an attempt to calm him. "Hear me out, please. I think you owe me that at least."

"*I owe you nothing!*"

Jessie, trying to appear unperturbed although her heart was pounding against her ribs so hard she imagined she could hear it, said in an even tone, "I will discuss your perceived grievances with Mr. Harrison and the other members of the Southern Pacific's board. I will not in-

67

form those gentlemen that you were the one who kidnapped me and wrote that note to Mr. Harrison. Perhaps I can persuade them to meet with you and any other representatives of the settlers you select to try to work things out in an amicable and rational fashion."

"Miss Starbuck, I've got to hand it to you. Like I said before, you talk like a Philadelphia lawyer, with your high-toned phrases like 'perceived grievances' and 'an amicable and rational fashion.' I don't know what half of those words mean. I haven't had the education you've obviously had. I went to a one-room schoolhouse in Tennessee before I came west to settle here, and half the time I couldn't attend because there were crops to plant or crops to cultivate or crops to harvest—"

Brandon muttered an oath under his breath. "Never mind about the sad story of my life. The answer is no. You stay here until such time as Ben Harrison sends word that he's caved in and is willing to go along with what we want."

And if he doesn't cave in? The question she had silently framed sent a chill through Jessie.

"You men are like mules sometimes," she said, watching Brandon watch her closely.

"You know a lot about men, do you?"

Jessie didn't miss the faintly erotic innuendo in Brandon's words that had been spoken with the ghost of a smirk. "I know they can be as insufferably stubborn as you are being at the moment, Mr. Brandon. I know that their stubbornness more often than not can be destructive to their avowed causes, whatever they might be. You have challenged Mr. Benjamin Harrison. What do you think his reaction to that challenge will be? Permit me the liberty of telling you what it will be. He will refuse to bend an inch in the face of what you are pleased to call your demands. The result: an impasse."

"You're leaving out one important ingredient. Yourself. I'm willing to go so far as to admit that maybe you have a point about my going about things in such a way as to get old Ben Harrison's back up. But he'll cool down soon enough when he thinks about the consequences of

68

him digging in his heels and refusing to budge. He won't want your blood on his hands.''

"You said a moment ago that you didn't understand some of the words I used. I don't believe that for a minute, Mr. Brandon. Not for one single minute do I believe that. I am, I like to think, a fairly good judge of men. I judge you to be not merely intelligent but above average in intelligence. So you can stop playing the country bumpkin with me. I think, Mr. Brandon, that you're intelligent enough to realize that Mr. Harrison may very well choose to put the interests of the Southern Pacific above my well-being. By that I mean he will view me as expendable if saving me might mean the damaging or the possible ruin of the railroad.''

"I don't see things the way you do, Miss Starbuck. I think Harrison won't want to read in the newspapers about how his failure to act in the face of a threat to one of his company's principal people led directly to that person's death. Do you think that kind of news will do the company any good? Don't bother to answer the question. It was rhetorical.''

Jessie couldn't resist the opportunity to taunt Brandon. "Now you are using words *I* don't understand. 'Rhetorical,' Mr. Brandon?''

He ignored her goading. "But even if Harrison is dumb enough or stupid enough to sacrifice you in order to maintain his and the railroad's position, there's a high card I've got left in my hand, which I will gladly play to win the game.''

"What, may I ask, is your high card?''

"If Harrison throws you to the wolves—''

"An interesting analogy, Mr. Brandon, '' Jessie interrupted.

"—what will he do when we kidnap *another* one of his board members? The papers will have a party with that news, I can guarantee you.'' Brandon intoned sonorously, pretending to quote a newspaper article, '' 'Jessie Starbuck now appears to have been only the first victim of an unknown group of kidnappers. Now another Southern Pacific executive has been kidnapped and threatened

69

with death if the railroad fails to meet the kidnappers' demands.' ''

"Mr. Brandon," Jessie declared angrily and a bit fearfully, "what you are doing and planning is pure folly. Folly that borders on madness."

"Call it what you damn well please," Brandon snarled and stormed out of the cabin.

Jessie remained where she was, not moving, but thinking fast. Could she? Did she dare?

She went to the window and looked out. At first she saw no sign of Mike Brandon, but then he moved into her range of vision as he marched back and forth in front of the cabin, his hands thrust into his pockets, his head lowered, a frown on his face. She looked both right and left. Trees on the left. Open grassland on the right.

She watched Brandon intently. She mentally measured the distance he walked in each direction before turning. Almost to the trees, turn, walk back. Toward the open ground where the round stone wall of the well stood. She moved to the door he had left open and watched him, standing just to one side so that he would not be able to see her. When he headed in the direction of the well again, she started to make her move.

But he turned unexpectedly and started back toward the trees, forcing her to step away from the doorway and out of his line of sight.

She waited, surreptitiously watching him.

He was on his way toward the well again, the trees behind him. Could she make it to the trees before he turned and saw her? There was only one way to find out. She took that way. She ran as fast as she could toward the trees, keeping to the grass and avoiding the wide stretch of rocky ground on her left. She wanted to look behind her but didn't pause long enough to do so. Hair flying out behind her, arms pumping, heart pounding, she ran on, the trees coming closer, closer . . .

She listened for the sound of her name being shouted by Brandon from behind her. She listened for the sound of his pounding footsteps as he pursued her. She heard neither.

Then, with an overwhelming sense of relief, she was in among the trees, which hid her from the world beyond the woods. She didn't stop running. Dodging tree trunks and ducking under low-hanging branches, she continued running, hating the sound of the crunching deadwood and other debris under her feet but powerless to do anything to stop the sound.

Her throat burned and her mouth was as dry as a desert. She desperately wanted to stop in order to catch her breath. But she didn't. She continued fleeing through the sun-dappled forest like a wild animal with the hounds at its heels, not daring to stop, not willing to succumb to the unnerving knowledge that she didn't know where she was going. The world around her was a blur of trees flashing past her and the wild flight of birds through their branches as if the birds were also fleeing for their lives as she was doing.

She had no sense of time. It was passing, she knew, but she did not know if she had been running for seconds, for minutes, or for hours. The sun on her left side was hot as she ran. . . .

She slowed her pace, her brow wrinkling. The sun *wasn't* on her left any longer. Now it was on her right. Which meant—

The knowledge struck her like a hammer blow. She had run in a circle through the woods. She was now racing back the way she had come. Toward the cabin. *Toward Mike Brandon!*

She turned swiftly, almost losing her balance in the act, and retraced her steps. On your left, she silently admonished herself. Be sure to keep the sun on your left. That way you'll know you're traveling in a relatively straight line *away* from the cabin.

Above her a blue jay screeched its annoyance at the invasion of its territory. She ignored it. But she did not ignore the sound she heard—or thought she heard— behind her. The sharp crack of breaking branches. She looked over her shoulder and saw, with immense relief, nothing. But then, only a few minutes later, she heard the sound again. It was louder now. She forced herself

71

to run faster, fearing as she did so that her lungs would burst. She narrowly missed colliding with the thick trunk of a tree that seemed to suddenly loom up directly in front of her.

Then, hard hands landed on her shoulders. They jerked her backward. She lost her balance and fell. Mike Brandon, who had seized her, fell heavily on top of her.

She struggled against him, fighting to get out from under him, as he gripped her wrists with his iron like fingers and pinioned her with her back to the ground. She raised her head, bared her teeth, and bit his left hand.

He gave a pained yelp and released his hold on her right wrist. She immediately began to pummel him—face, chest, shoulders. But to no avail. He simply took the blows with a broad smile that infuriated her.

"You should have known I'd catch you," he said in his deep voice that seemed even deeper since his face was now so close to hers.

Her head fell back and hit the ground with a soft thud. She closed her eyes, the fight gone out of her temporarily. She lay there, concentrating on getting her breath and her strength back. But her concentration was soon broken as she became keenly aware of the heat of Brandon's body pressing so hard against her own. She could hear his breathing, which was almost as rapid and shallow as her own. Then she felt his lips on hers—and she twisted her head to one side to avoid them.

But Brandon was not to be deterred by such tactics, as she quickly discovered. He merely gripped her jaw in one hand and forcibly turned her head back toward him. Again his lips were on hers and again she turned her head—tried to—but found she could not do so because his fingers gripped her jaw so tightly she could not move her head. She gritted her teeth and pressed her lips together. It worked. His lips left hers.

She stared up at him and was about to speak when she felt his body shift atop hers. Then she felt something else, and she knew that he was fully aroused. There was, she noticed, a wild look in his eyes. His lips were slightly parted and his breath made a faint hissing sound as it left his mouth.

She swung her free right hand. It struck his cheek and left a red mark where it had landed.

As she raised her hand to strike him again, he easily slapped it to one side and then encircled both of her wrists with his left hand, leaving her helpless to defend herself. Her body tensed as she felt him move his right leg purposefully. She tried to keep her own legs together but he succeeded in nudging them apart, bit by bit, until his own legs lay on the ground between her spread ones.

He kissed her again, still holding her jaw to keep her from turning her head away from him. She made no response. Her eyes widened in surprise as his hand suddenly withdrew from her jaw. She wanted to turn her head away from him before he could try to kiss her again. She wanted . . .

Brandon, as if he knew of or could sense her eager wanting, began to kiss her cheeks, her nose, her throat. His wet tongue tickled her. At first. Then it aroused her. She tried to push it away with her own tongue when Brandon thrust it into her mouth, but another part of her, one that was rapidly becoming as aroused as Brandon himself so obviously was, made her refrain from doing so. It was that desire-ridden part of her that demanded she surrender to this man who, despite their relationship of kidnapper to kidnapped, through some mysterious power he seemed to possess, was making her want him as much as he apparently wanted her.

She stopped trying to force his tongue from her mouth. She tentatively touched it with her own. Then her lips closed on his tongue and she began to suck it. As he released his hold on her—but only his purely *physical* hold—his hands slid between their bodies and began to caress her breasts.

Her ardor, her desire for him, intensified.

Abruptly he withdrew his tongue from her mouth, and she felt, oddly, as if its withdrawal was more of a violation than its invasion had been. Involuntarily, she raised

73

her head slightly as she had done before. But this time she was seeking his lips, his tongue, his kiss . . .

"Are you ready," he asked her, his voice husky.

She recognized the question for what it was: a request that she surrender to him.

"Are you ready?" he asked a second time, and she, capitulating to the man who had mastered her in a defeat that was somehow glorious, meekly answered, "Yes, I'm ready."

And she was. She could feel her juices flowing, a testament to Brandon's ability to arouse her.

There was a fumbling with clothes then for both of them. Buttons were undone. Garments were pulled up and pulled down. Their coming together was a forceful thing. They coupled like two creatures incomplete in themselves and desperately needing the other one to perfect their existence.

Brandon thrust his extraordinarily large and tumescent member into Jessie, and she received him with a satisfied grunt, her arms encircling him and her legs wrapping themselves around his muscular thighs.

He immediately began to buck, his strong hands gripping Jessie's shoulders, his face buried against her neck. She matched his wild rhythm willingly, and the sensations that flowed through her made her entire body tremble with delight and desire. She held on to him as if she had made up her mind never to let him go. As if she would never let him leave her. She made a conscious effort to tighten her grip on his erection, and as she did so he gave a long drawn-out moan of pleasure.

He slowed his movements, swiveling his hips slightly, and evoking a groan from Jessie, whose fingernails bit into his back.

He raised his head, and then, propping himself up on his hands, he stared down at her as he probed, withdrew from her—but not all the way—and then plunged deep inside her again.

She cried out shrilly, her voice startling a squirrel on an overhead branch and sending it scurrying away out of sight. She gloried in his sexual teasing, which was bringing her rapidly toward a climax. When he would begin to withdraw from her, she would slam her pelvis upward to embrace him and then sink down when he lowered the weight of his loins upon her once more.

She drew a deep breath and then let it out in a series of sighs as she climaxed and Brandon continued pumping his shaft into her. She held him tightly and knew he, too, had climaxed when he suddenly began to shudder and mutter, "Oh, good, so good, so damned *good!*"

They were still for several minutes afterward, locked in an embrace, their bodies still melded tightly together. Then, almost imperceptibly, Jessie began to stir beneath Brandon. Within seconds she was rocking under him, her hips swirling in an erotic circle. He let her do all the work for several minutes, and then he, too, began to participate in what she was doing. They pleasured each other in a way that surprised them both and led quickly and surely to a second climax for each of them. It left them both spent but satisfied.

Gradually, as their passion drained away, reality returned. Brandon pulled out of Jessie and began to straighten his clothes. She sat up and proceeded to do the same.

"Let's go," he said curtly, getting to his feet and gesturing peremptorily.

She got up, and he pointed out the direction they were to take.

Jessie walked ahead of him, her head held high, still the proud beauty unwilling to utter the first word concerning what had just happened between them.

"I didn't mean for that to happen," he said from behind her.

"Neither did I."

"It doesn't change anything between us."

Jessie wasn't so sure about that. But she made up her mind to bide her time to see if Brandon's remark was indeed the truth or was just a way for him to hide his feelings from her in order to proceed with his plan to force the railroad to reconsider its policies.

"Hey, there, Mike!" one of a pair of men called out

as Brandon and Jessie emerged from the woods near the cabin a few minutes later. "We wondered what had happened to you."

"She decided to make a run for it, Bill," Brandon said. "She caught me off guard."

Jessie recognized the man Brandon had spoken to as the one who had helped him disrupt the stockholders' meeting in San Francisco.

"How are you, Isaac?" Brandon shook hands with the other man, who was gaunt and mustachioed and whose gray eyes were on Jessie.

"So this is the famous Miss Starbuck," he said. "Bill told me you'd—uh, brought her here with you."

"Miss Starbuck," Brandon said flatly, "This is Bill Fowler, who you know or at least heard from at your meeting, and Isaac Pendleton, president of our local lodge of the National Grange of the Patrons of Husbandry. Two men who, like me and a whole lot of other people, are bound and determined to bring your railroad to its knees."

"Mike has a way of speaking melodramatically at times, Miss Starbuck," Pendleton remarked. "We don't want to bring the railroad to its knees—*I* don't, at any rate. What I do want is to make it stop its many harmful practices that hurt farmers, such as the exorbitant terminal rate and its unfair habit of giving rebates to big shippers and soaking the small farmers to make up for them."

"I have been trying to tell Mr. Brandon," Jessie said, "that he cannot hope to prevail if he insists on using such tactics as kidnapping. He will only incur the wrath of the men charged with running the Southern Pacific railroad, not their cooperation."

"We have suffered much for a long time, Miss Starbuck," Pendleton declared. "We feel the time has come for drastic action. Drastic action of the kind Mike has taken in your case."

"Mike, there's a fellow in town asking a lot of questions about you. He seems hell-bent on finding you."

76

"Do you think he's an agent of the railroad?" Brandon asked.

"He may very well be," Fowler said.

"What does he look like?" Brandon asked.

"He's Chinese or Japanese or something," Fowler answered. "But taller than most Orientals. He looks like he might be part white."

Jessie's heart leaped as the men continued talking about Ki. She tried not to let her expression change. Her face remained impassive, but her skin tingled.

"It might be a good idea to get him out of our way," Fowler suggested. "I don't like the idea of some stranger asking questions about you, Mike. The railroad knows you're our ramrod. We could be in for trouble."

Jessie's composure cracked. "Don't do anything to hurt him!" she cried. "The man you're talking about is a friend of mine. His name is Ki. I'm sure he's come here to look for me."

"There you go, Mike," Fowler said. "You heard her. The man means trouble for us. Do you want me to take care of him?"

Jessie turned to Brandon, her eyes pleading with him.

He hesitated a moment and then said, "Don't do anything, Bill. Just steer clear of him. We'll all steer clear of him till this thing's settled once and for all."

"Have it your way, Mike," Fowler said. "I'll leave him alone. But as you well know, there are a few hotheads amongst us. Maybe one of them will get his dander up and decide to put a stop to this fellow's pesky questions and his snooping around."

"Let's go inside," Brandon said. "I've got to tether the lady nice and tight so she doesn't try to make another run for it again any time soon."

Chapter 5

The drink Ki had ordered from the bar dog at the Groveland saloon remained untouched on the oak bar in front of him as he scanned the room and the people in it.

Two hardcases playing poker at a table in the corner. A drunk sleeping it off, his head resting on his arms, which were splayed out on the table before him. A man and a woman, the woman looking bored, the man looking lustful.

Ki turned his attention to the bar dog who was busily washing glasses and stacking them on a wooden drainboard.

"How has Mike Brandon been doing in his long-running battle with the Southern Pacific?" he asked the man.

The bar dog looked up from the sudsy water in which his arms were immersed up to their knobby elbows. He looked down again, not bothering to answer the question.

"That Brandon," Ki continued, "he's turning out to be a legend in his own time. I've heard tell of him all up and down the line. In every town, village, and hamlet. Folks think he's some kind of hero. What do you think?"

"I think people who ask too many questions wind up in a peck of trouble."

"I'm just trying to be friendly." Eyeing the bar dog, Ki added, "I'd like to be friendly with Mike Brandon— if I could find him. In fact, I'd like to lend him a hand if he'll let me. I'm no railroad lover, not by a long shot. When they evicted me from my land last week, that was the straw that broke this camel's back, I can tell you. But I'm not taking it lying down. I'm going to get my revenge, one way or another."

"You say you were evicted last week?"

Well, at least I've got his interest with my lies, Ki thought. "That's right."

"Where was your land?"

"Right here in Fresno County."

"Whereabouts in Fresno County exactly?"

Ki looked down at his glass, avoiding the bar dog's suspicious gaze. Where exactly? He didn't know the county, had no idea where to say his land had been. "East of town," he finally answered, hoping his reply would satisfy the bar dog.

It didn't.

"Was it near the Hendersons' homestead?"

I've got a fifty-fifty chance of giving the right answer, Ki thought. "Yes, it was, as a matter of fact," he tried.

"You're a liar, mister," the bar dog said loud enough to spark the interest of the other people in the saloon. "There's no Henderson homestead anywhere east of Groveland or in any other direction around here, either. What's your game?"

"I'm playing no game," Ki said quietly. "I guess I got my directions mixed up. I never worked the land myself, you see. I rented it out to tenant farmers."

"Are you a railroad agent out after Mike Brandon?" the bar dog barked, drying his hands with a dirty cloth and glaring at Ki.

"No, I'm not." Ki rose. "I didn't come in here to mix it up with anybody, but it seems like that's what you've got in mind to do. Being a peaceable man, I'm backing off right now."

As Ki turned to go, he found himself facing the two poker-playing hardcases he had noticed earlier, who had come up behind him.

"Got trouble with this fellow, Simon?" the burlier of the two men asked the bar dog.

"He's asking questions about Mike Brandon, Dade."

"Well, maybe Rio and me can answer them for him. What do you want to know about Brandon, mister?"

Ki swiftly considered his options. He could cut and run. Or he could stand his ground and maybe bluff his way into obtaining the information—some of it, at least—that he was seeking.

"I was just telling your friend, Simon, here about my heartfelt admiration for Mike Brandon. I was saying I'd like to shake the man's hand and throw in with him if he'll let me. But I don't know where to find him."

"Neither do we," the man named Rio snapped, "so go find somebody who does know where Mike's at."

"I think I'll do that, and I hope whoever I find turns out to be a whole lot friendlier than the people I've talked to so far here in Groveland."

Dade and Rio exchanged glances as Ki stepped around them and headed for the batwings. He had almost reached them when he spun around, sensing they were coming up on him from behind. He planted his feet firmly apart and raised his hands. "I don't want any trouble," he said.

"Neither do we," Rio said, "but it appears you've come to town to make it."

"We're going to nip it in the bud before it gets out of hand," Dade announced. He lunged at Ki, who neatly sidestepped and brought his hand down on the back of Dade's neck, sending the man stumbling through the batwings and out onto the street.

Ki was ready when Rio moved in on him, both hands angrily reaching for his throat. Ki crooked his right arm and then flung it outward. His hand at the end of his outthrust arm caught Rio in the throat and almost shattered the man's windpipe.

Gagging and clutching his throat, Rio staggered back-

81

ward. He bent over and vomited on the sawdust-strewn floor. As Ki was about to turn and leave the saloon, he heard the batwings swing open behind him. Two arms went around him from behind in a bear hug that almost emptied his lungs of air.

"Get up Rio, you dumb son of a bitch!" Dade yelled from behind Ki as he held his captive immobile. "Give it to him now while I've got him so he can't fight back. *Do it*, Rio!"

Rio took a step toward Ki, who remained motionless in Dade's iron grip. On his face was a look of such pure hatred that Ki was almost forced to look away from him.

Rio took another step. "Hold him, Dade. Don't let him loose. He's hell with all the fences down when he has a chance to be."

Another step and then Rio wound up and let his right fist fly.

Ki responded by letting his total body weight drop, which enabled him to slide down in Dade's arms, which were still gripping him. Simultaneously he brought both of his arms up to further weaken Dade's bear hug, and he thrust his right hand at Rio's eyes, startling Rio and causing him to duck and step backward in order to protect himself.

Which gave Ki sufficient time to ram his right elbow into Dade's solar plexus. The blow had the desired effect of temporarily paralyzing Dade's diaphragm so that he could not breathe. Then Ki dropped down into the martial arts move known as a Deep Horse and rammed the pommel—his right fist—into Dade's testicles, temporarily disabling his attacker and completely breaking the man's hold on him.

He repeated the movement he had used to strike Rio earlier, and again the man staggered backward, clutching his throat and sounding as if he was choking to death.

Ki pivoted clockwise, turning his attention once again to Dade. He gave the man a downward chop on the back of the neck, which dropped Dade to the floor. Then he brought his right foot up and kicked Rio in the face, knocking the man senseless.

82

He drew a deep breath, turned, and went through the batwings without a backward glance.

He made his way to the livery barn, where after the farrier had greeted him pleasantly, he said, "I'd like to rent a good horse and the gear to go on him."

"I've got two you can pick from," the farrier said. "They're out back in a corral."

The two men went to the corral, where Ki spent several minutes examining the two mounts in the enclosure. The buckskin mare was swaybacked and a kicker, but the black stallion with the blaze looked sturdy enough. Big-brisketed. Smooth shiny coat. Clear eyes. Two, maybe three years old.

"How much?" Ki asked, pointing at the black.

After a minute or two of the customary haggling, Ki and the farrier settled on a price for the mount and gear, and a little while after that Ki led the saddled and bridled black out of the livery.

Time to play my only ace, he thought as he swung into the saddle and rode out of town, heading west, unaware of Rio and Dade standing unsteadily outside the saloon and watching him. If it—if she—really is an ace and doesn't turn out to be as close-mouthed and mean as just about everybody else I've talked to about the whereabouts of Mike Brandon. But she might figure she owes me a favor for what I did to help her when Jessie and I stopped off in Groveland on our way to San Francisco.

As image of Helen Simmons drifted through his mind, bringing a small smile to his face. A lovely woman, he thought. Had a smile as bright as sunshine. Had a body . . .

He pushed the thought aside. He had no time for such thoughts or, for that matter, for the behavior that such thoughts usually led to. His visit to Helen Simmons would be strictly business. Time was passing and Jessie . . . He didn't want to think about what might be happening to Jessie. What might have already happened to Jessie.

He scanned the horizon as he rode, looking for signs

of habitation. Helen Simmons, he recalled, had mentioned that she lived three miles west of town. He estimated that he had already covered a good two miles. Not much farther to go.

The shot that whipped past the left side of his head caused his horse to falter and try to bolt. He maintained a tight grip on the reins and looked over his shoulder. Two men in the distance behind him. Two men with guns in their hands. Two men, he saw, as they galloped closer to him, named Dade and Rio.

Bad pennies, he thought wryly. They keep showing up. But these two bad pennies weren't just nuisances. They were dangerous. Because of the six-guns they had in their hands. Ki put heels to his horse and went racing away from them, wondering where they had gotten the guns or if they had had them all the time during the battle in the bar. But he'd seen no sign of weapons then. Never mind. They had them now. That's what mattered.

Another round whined past Ki, barely missing his shoulder. He bent down low over his horse's neck to make himself as small a target as possible and rode on, whipping his mount with his reins.

A feeling of relief washed over him when he saw a thin swirl of smoke rising in the distance. Shelter up ahead. Good, since there's not even a tree to take cover behind out here on the plain.

The third round plowed into his back and almost knocked him off his horse. He felt as if he had been hit with a nine-pound sledge. Then, for an odd moment, he felt nothing. No pain. No hot blood flowing down his back from his wound. But then, suddenly and with the impact of a battering ram, pain came crashing down upon him. His upper torso felt as if it were on fire. He had difficulty remaining upright. He also had difficulty staying in the saddle because of a feeling of weakness that threatened to overcome him.

A sod house up ahead.

Its outlines blurred, and Ki knew that he was on the verge of losing consciousness. The soddy regained its solid shape. He blinked, trying hard to keep the building in focus. Behind him, the sound of hoofbeats had grown louder, meaning that his pair of pursuers was gaining on him. He turned the black sharply so that its body was at right angles to the two men behind him. At the same time that he turned the animal, he let his body slide down, Indian-fashion, so that the horse was between him and Dade and Rio. Hanging on to his saddle horn with one hand, he brought the horse to a halt not far from the soddy. His feet slid out of the stirrups, and then he was crouching with his feet on the ground and his hand still on his saddle horn to steady the black, which was nervously trying to circle.

Two more shots sounded.

But they had not come from the guns of Rio or Dade. These had been rounds fired from a double-barreled shotgun. Out of the corner of his eye, Ki watched Helen Simmons lower the gun in her hands after firing the two warning shots into the air and level the weapon at Dade and Rio, who quickly drew rein some forty yards away from the soddy.

"How come you're shooting at us, Miss Simmons?" an indignant Dade called out. "We're after him, not you." He pointed at Ki, who had straightened up but still stood with his horse between him and the two men.

"I can see that," Helen Simmons responded. "But I want no shooting on my place—especially not at an unarmed man. I want you both to turn around and ride on out of here."

"Ma'am, you don't seem to understand," Rio said, his voice on the edge of a whine. "This fellow was in town stirring up trouble for us settlers."

"*Us* settlers?" Helen shot back. "Since when are you two settlers? All you've done is camped out on that empty land that the Boone family abandoned some time back."

"We been fighting the good fight right alongside your brother and Mike Brandon, Miss Simmons," Dade declared. "And like Rio just said, that fellow there, he's bent on making trouble for all of us—your brother included along with Brandon."

"My brother can take care of himself. So can Mike

85

Brandon. Are you going to leave, or am I going to make you leave?''

"He jumped us in town," Rio said, pointing at Ki. "So we went and got our guns and set out to trail him. He means harm to all of us around here, ma'am. So why don't you put down that iron you're toting and let us get even with him for the things he did to us? By the time we're through with him, he won't be able to cause any of us any harm."

Helen thumbed back the hammers on her shotgun.

Dade and Rio exchanged glances and then Dade said, "You're making a bad move, Miss Simmons."

"One that you, and maybe the rest of us as well, will wind up being sorry for," Rio added.

Helen said nothing; she merely stood her ground, the shotgun steady in her hands.

Reluctantly both men turned their horses and rode away.

Helen waited until they were almost out of sight, and then she propped the shotgun against the wall of the soddy and hurried over to Ki, who was hanging on to his saddle horn with both hands now to keep from falling.

"Are you all right—I don't know your name. When we met, you didn't tell me your name. Sir?"

"My name—it's Ki."

"You're hurt. Let me help you inside."

"I can make it." But Ki found that was not true as he let go of the saddle horn and took a step toward the house. He would have fallen had not Helen put an arm around his waist and draped his right arm over her shoulders. Walking slowly, the pair made it to the soddy and then inside it. Helen helped Ki into a bedroom and over to a bed that stood against a wall.

"I can't lie down there," he murmured, his vision growing dim. "I'll bleed all over—"

"Never mind about that. Here. Let me help you lie down."

But before Helen could do so, Ki fainted from loss of blood and fell face forward onto the brightly patterned quilt covering the bed.

• • •

The next morning Jessie awoke from a fitful slumber to the sound of low voices conversing on the far side of the room. She opened her eyes and for a moment wasn't sure where she was. But then, at her first sight of the cabin's rude walls and the two men sharing it with her, she knew where she was and where she wished she wasn't. She lay on the bed where she had spent the night, her left wrist tied with a length of rope which ran under the bed where it had been tied to the bed's spring. She tried to stretch to rid her body of the aches that her confinement had caused her during the long night but could not do so with any kind of ease. She settled for rolling her shoulders to loosen the muscles in them as she listened to what Mike Brandon was saying to Bill Fowler, who had also spent the night in the cabin.

"The railroad's given Matt Cornell and his family until today to either pay for the land they've been farming for close to four years now or get out. I talked to Matt before we went to San Francisco, and he sounded to me as if he was on the verge of throwing in the towel."

"He's going to let them evict him?" Fowler asked.

Brandon nodded. "That's how he sounded to me. I tried my damnedest to talk him out of it, but the problem is talk's cheap and the land's dear. Matt hasn't got the cash to pay for it, so my talk can't keep him on the land. Only cold cash will do that, and Matt doesn't think he can raise it."

"You'd think the railroad would give us terms, wouldn't you? Let us pay so much down and so much a month."

"They want cash on the barrelhead, and by God, they've been getting it. But not from a lot of the settlers around here who just plain don't have that kind of money. They've been getting it from speculators who come in and buy the land, sell the crops on it come harvesttime, and then unload the land at a tidy profit. The railroad's just not about to wait for their money, damn them."

"It's always the same old story," Fowler commented,

his voice mournful. "Those that have the wherewithal and those that don't."

"Before Isaac left here yesterday, he told me he'd been talking to Matt," said Brandon, "and Matt said he thought he might try again to talk the bank into giving him a note that would let him buy his land. Matt told Isaac he was going into town to talk to Mr. Peters at the bank. I've got a notion to ride over to Matt's place and see how things stand with him at this point. Maybe he got the money. If he didn't, well, at least I'll get a chance to bid him good-bye before he pulls up stakes and takes off."

"What are you going to do about her?" Fowler gestured in Jessie's direction.

"Are you needed at home, Bill?"

"No. Why? You want me to stay here and keep an eye on her while you're over to Matt's?"

"Can you see your way clear to do that?"

"Sure, I can. You go on. Tell Matt and the missus I'm sorry for their trouble, and I hope it turns out that this cloud hanging over them somehow or other turns out to have a silver lining."

Brandon rose and crossed the room. Looking down at Jessie, he asked, "You ready for some breakfast?"

"Not if breakfast means another helping of that greasy sowbelly we had for supper last night, I'm not."

"Beggers can't be choosers."

"I'm not begging you for anything, Mr. Brandon."

"Suit yourself."

As Jessie recalled the unpleasantly greasy taste of the sowbelly Brandon had served her the night before, a thought suddenly occurred to her. "I've changed my mind, Mr. Brandon. I will have a helping of sowbelly if it's not too much trouble."

"You heard the lady, Bill," Brandon said.

"You don't want any breakfast, Mike?"

"I'll pass this time. Be back soon as I can so you can get on home."

"Take your time. I'm in no hurry."

When Brandon had gone, Jessie said, "I have to relieve myself."

Fowler, who was busy with a skillet and a slab of sowbelly, glanced at her. Then he crossed the room and proceeded to untie the rope that bound her to the bed. "Don't try anything cute, you hear? If you do, I'll have to stop you. I don't want to hurt you, but I will if you force me to."

Jessie waited in silence while he finished untying the rope and then, rubbing her wrist, which was raw from the rope's chafing, she left the cabin with Fowler right behind her.

"I'd like a little privacy," she told him.

"I've got none to give you. You might try to run off if I let you out of my sight for so much as a second. Go on. Do whatever it is you have to do."

A resigned Jessie walked behind a bush.

When she was finished, she rejoined Fowler as a light rain began to fall. He escorted her back to the cabin, where he retied her left wrist to the bedsprings, from which she could not free herself without attracting Fowler's attention. But there was, she believed, a way to break free without calling attention to herself.

"Not so tight," she protested.

He ignored her as he knotted the rope in place.

Later, when he placed a tin plate of boiled beans and sowbelly on the bed beside her, she looked at the meal with distaste but took the fork he handed her and proceeded to eat the beans, which were still hard, and the sowbelly, which was far too greasy for her taste.

From time to time she glanced at Fowler, who was sitting at the wooden table in the center of the room, idly flipping the pages of a Montgomery Ward catalog as he ate his own breakfast with obvious relish.

She shifted position so that her body was between Fowler and the plate resting on the bed. She put down her fork and picked up a piece of sowbelly. Surreptitiously, she began to rub the meat on the rope that bound her wrist to the bed frame. She worked swiftly and silently, coating the rope with grease from the meat. Then

89

she rubbed more grease above and below the spot where the rope encircled her wrist and also on her hand and fingers.

"What do you think of that!" Fowler exclaimed, causing Jessie to stop what she was doing and turn to face him.

"This Monkey Ward outfit's got everything under the sun for sale. Even something called a Doctor Ames's porous plaster that's guaranteed, it says right here in black and white, to pull pain out of any portion of a person's body or your money cheerfully refunded. I could sure use one of those porous plasters. I've had a trick knee ever since I fell off my horse last Christmas Eve 'cause I'd had me a cup or two too many of the oh-be-joyful. It aches sometime fierce every time it rains."

Jessie made no comment.

"And look here. They got a tonic for sale. An iron Kola and Celery Compound Tonic. It says it's a 'System Tonic and Body Builder—Recommended for Men, Women, and Children.' It's got everything in it but the kitchen sink, it appears. 'Boneset Herb, Sienna, Rhubarb, Iron Citrate in Cherry Wine,' and a whole lot of other stuff. It sounds to me like this stuff might kill you if it doesn't cure you."

Jessie waited until Fowler was once again immersed in silent study of the wonders contained in the mail order catalog before resuming her efforts to free herself. When she was satisfied that she had thoroughly coated the rope with grease, she began to twist and turn her wrist in an attempt to free her hand. But the rope held. It did slide a little, but not enough for her to pull her hand free.

Still, she kept at it, unwilling to give up. She pulled, straining against the unyielding rope, until the tendons in her wrist began to pain her. She tried turning her wrist as far as she could in one direction and then reversing direction. The sowbelly grease, warmed by the heat of her blood, began to drip down onto the bed.

"They want two ninety-five for a pair of Levis's," Fowler said, his remark made almost inaudible by the booming of thunder as the rain intensified. "That's highway robbery, if you ask me,'' he muttered around his mouthful of beans.

Jessie, as she warily watched Fowler, felt the rope slide up over her hand. She turned her head slowly, straining against the rope, and saw that it had slipped almost halfway up her hand. Encouraged by this sign of progress, she redoubled her efforts, glancing back at Fowler every few seconds so that he wouldn't be able to come up on her unexpectedly and discover what she was doing.

She picked up another piece of sowbelly and vigorously rubbed it on her hand. Squeezing her fingers into as tight a space as she could possibly manage, she tried again, pulling as hard as she could.

The rope slid up and over and off her hand. She almost let out a yell of victory. Instead, she forced herself to remain calm. She kept her supposedly still-bound hand hidden behind her as she twisted her body and scanned the room, looking for something, she wasn't sure what.

Her eyes fell and fastened on the three-legged stool that sat next to the hearth. She calculated the distance between it and her, calculated whether or not she could make a dash for it and get it in her hand before Fowler could react. Maybe. Maybe not. But it was the only thing in the room she could easily use for the purpose she had in mind.

She wiped the grease from her hand as she sat without moving on the bed, her eyes shifting from the stool to Fowler and back again. When her hand was finally free of fat, she made her move. She was up off the bed in an instant and bounding across the room. Seconds later, as Fowler, his mouth hanging open in stunned surprise and his catalog completely forgotten, started to rise and reach for her, she seized the stool, spun around, and swung it.

But before it could strike him on the head, Fowler threw up his right arm and blocked it. The stool gave his shoulder a glancing blow, which was severe enough to make him cry out in pain.

Jessie lost her balance when the stool struck, and she

almost fell. With a roar of rage Fowler lunged for her. He managed to seize her right wrist, but his hand slipped on the faint residue of grease that still coated it, and he lost his grip on her.

Jessie raised the stool above her head, intending to bring it crashing down on her captor. But the lithe Fowler saw the blow coming and neatly sidestepped it. At the same time that the stool came flying downward, he made a grab for Jessie, but she, bringing the stool up even faster than she had just brought it down, struck him on the forearm with it. The blow sent him spinning away from her, and as he did so, she raced for the door. Throwing it open and the stool aside, she fled from the cabin into the pouring rain outside.

She quickly freed the reins of Fowler's horse, which were wrapped around a hitch rail near the cabin door, and swung into the saddle. Jerking the reins to turn the horse sharply, she slammed her heels into its flanks. The animal, a bay, went galloping away from the cabin just as an enraged Fowler came running out of it.

"Stop!" he yelled at the fleeing Jessie. "*Stop, god-dammit!*"

She didn't stop or even slow down. She had no intention of stopping until she put many miles between her and Fowler and maybe not even then. She galloped through the pouring rain that plastered her hair to her head and her mount's mane to its sleek neck. With no sun to guide her, she wasn't sure in which direction she was heading. She decided it didn't matter. All that mattered, at least at the present moment, was to get away from Fowler. Once she was able to get her bearings, she would find a town and from there head back to San Francisco aboard the Southern Pacific.

She rode on through the rain and the occasional thunder, which was inevitably followed by streaks of yellow lightning that did little to brighten the gloom of the sunless day. The sky was the color of lead. The rain was gray and cold. The world through which Jessie rode seemed to lack even the slightest bit of color.

But it didn't lack for sound. Thunder continued to

cannonade through the valley, loud enough to hurt a listener's ears. But Jessie paid no attention to it. Nor did she pay attention to the fact that her clothes were soaking wet. These minor disturbances were of no import to her. What did matter to her was the fact that she had accomplished what she had set out to do. She had escaped from the cabin. She hoped she would never see Bill Fowler or Mike Brandon again.

The thought had barely crossed her mind when she found herself revising it somewhat. She wouldn't mind seeing Mike Brandon again. Under the right circumstances. If the world changed, and she and he were not on the opposite sides of a conflict that was tearing the area apart. But that situation had little chance or hope of changing, she thought. Not when Brandon was capable of resorting to such drastic tactics as kidnapping to gain an advantage for the side he represented. She was surprised to find that she felt no resentment toward the man for his kidnapping and subsequent imprisoning of her. Part of her understood his motives and, secretly, admired both them and his adventurous actions which had grown out of them.

She tried to make herself hate Brandon. Or at least dislike him. To her surprise, she could do neither.

She rode past a large herd of cattle that had apparently been put out to pasture on a vast stretch of lush grassland. The animals were beginning to mill as the rain pelted them. They moved slowly in a circle, blinking the rain from their large brown eyes.

Jessie, noting the animals' restlessness as they milled, turned and rode off at right angles to the herd, intending to get as far away from them as she could. A milling herd was, she knew, both unpredictable and potentially dangerous.

She had not gone far when thunder again roared through the valley. It was followed seconds later by a brilliant flash of jagged lightning that struck a locust tree off to her right and sent it crashing to the ground. Another thunderclap. More lightning.

She heard them before she saw them.

The hooves of the loudly bawling cattle pounded the ground as they began to mill in an ever-widening circle.

Jessie glanced over her shoulder and squinted, trying to see through the sheets of rain that were blurring her vision. The cattle, frightened by the thunder and the tree the lightning had toppled, broke out of their mill and began to run in a straight line.

Jessie, urging her horse onward, raced away from the herd heading toward her. They, as if not wanting to be left behind, continued to run after her, their huge horned heads swinging from side to side, their hooves throwing mud in every direction.

Stampede!

The dread word numbed Jessie's mind.

But it did not numb her muscles. Or her will to save herself from the oncoming horde of cattle.

She whipped her horse with the reins, urging it to move faster, willing it to *fly*. The bay responded gamely under the lash. It sped forward, its head bobbing almost violently and its ears erect, as it splashed through puddles the size of little lakes and over unstable ground that threatened to bog it down at any moment.

Behind her the cattle had grown ominously silent. They no longer bawled as they fled the frights unleashed by the sky—the thunder and lightning that had so terrorized them. But Jessie could hear the clatter and clash of their horns striking one another. A harsh symphony straight out of hell.

As the rain continued to fall, the day darkened even more.

Jessie spotted a large grove of trees standing like leafy sentinels ahead of her on the left. If she could reach them in time, she could ride in among them, and thus have a good chance of avoiding the unthinkable fate of being trampled to death beneath the hooves of the oncoming cattle. She made a split-second decision to head for the trees, although to reach them she had to swerve to the left at a forty-five degree angle, which, she knew, would make her more vulnerable to the stampeding cattle than she would be if she had continued to race ahead of them

in a straight line. But it was a chance she felt she had
to take for the simple reason that it was the only chance
available to her to escape an impending bloody death.

The bay beneath her began to slow. She tried to flog
it into another spurt of speed but couldn't. She was not
surprised. The animal's breath was coming in ragged
spurts now, and she could feel its sides heaving with the
valiant efforts it was making to respond to her commands.

But she couldn't slow down. She had to get to those
trees and get there before the cattle, close behind her
now, could reach her.

The grove was, she estimated, only fifty yards ahead
of her now. A few moments later only forty yards. Then
thirty.

Her horse suddenly stumbled and broke stride. She
felt it going before it actually went down. Then, as the
animal pitched forward, she leaped from the saddle.

She hit the ground running. Running for her life toward
the trees still so heartbreakingly far away while behind
her the bay struggled gamely to its feet and then fled in
the opposite direction to try to escape, as Jessie was
doing, the oncoming herd of cattle.

Jessie's heart pounded in her chest as she ran and the
rain pelted her unmercifully. Her chest heaved with the
effort. Blood drummed in her brain. Her world had narrowed to a single focus, and that focus was the trees now
seeming to grow taller and taller as she came closer to
them.

Her legs ached with the effort of her frantic race for
life because the boggy ground sucked at her feet and
made running difficult.

But she persevered, the clanging of the cattle's huge
horns a goad forcing her forward. She imagined she could
feel the hot breath of the huge beasts on her back. She
began to fear that her legs would give out on her and
she would fall . . .

As a sycamore tree loomed up before her, she didn't
think; she simply acted. She sprang upward, straining
with all her might to free herself from the soggy ground
underfoot, her arms stretched high above her head. Her

fingers closed on the lowest limb of the sycamore, and her feet left the ground. Her body swung forward and then back. She managed to pull herself up onto the sycamore's limb and she lay prone upon it, her arms and legs wrapped tightly around it as thunder roared in the sky and thunder also roared on the ground—the ground-thunder made by hundreds of hooves pounding past.

Jessie stared transfixed as the mass of tightly packed steers went racing beneath the tree and beyond it. The flood of shaggy bodies continued passing beneath the sycamore for what seemed to Jessie to be an eternity. At one point, as the rapid pace of the cattle held steady and more animals crowded into the limited space between the trees, several steers were slammed up against the sycamore where Jessie had taken refuge. As the tree shook, Jessie tightened her grip on it, praying that its roots wouldn't give way to send her crashing down to the ground and to a horrible death beneath the relentless hooves of the stampeding herd.

★

Chapter 6

Ki awoke from a fitful sleep that had been haunted by distressing dreams of Jessie calling out to him to come and help her, and he, although he could hear her, could not see her and thus could not come to her aid.

He lay in the unfamiliar bed that no longer bore the bright quilt on which he remembered bleeding the day before and let the morning sunshine bathe him in its welcome warmth.

But he could not stay where he was. He had to get up. First, however, he had to talk to Helen Simmons to see if she could give him any information that would help him find Jessie. He glanced at his clothes, which were draped over a chair next to the bed.

"I see you're awake."

He turned his head and gazed at Helen, who was standing in the doorway of the bedroom and looking lovely with the sun on her blond hair and fair skin. "I'm awake."

"I thought you were going to sleep the day away as well as the night just passed," she said, coming over to the bed and placing the back of her hand against his forehead. "No fever," she said. "The doctor told me to watch to see if you become feverish."

"I thank you for bringing the doctor to me, Helen."

"I thought I would never see you again when we parted following our first meeting. Then you turned up on my doorstep yesterday with those two rowdies hot on your heels. I can tell you that was quite a surprise."

"But it wasn't an accident. I was on my way to pay you a visit when those two gunslingers turned up on my trail."

Helen gave Ki an appraising look. "I'm flattered that you wanted to see me again. I shan't ask why. Not now. But I will after you've had some breakfast. What would you like? I've fresh eggs and some roast ham I can heat up. You must be hungry."

"I feel like I'm on the verge of starving to death. Anything you can put together without too much trouble will suit me fine."

"I'll be back soon."

When Helen had gone, Ki lay on the bed with his eyes closed, basking in the sunshine and feeling guilty about what he was doing. I should be up and out of here and to hell with breakfast, he told himself. But he consoled himself with the hope that Helen Simmons would be able to provide him with information he could use in his continuing hunt for Jessie.

He gingerly touched the bandage that covered his shoulder wound that the doctor Helen had brought to the soddy had tended to the day before. It still ached, but the pain was considerably less than it had been when he had been shot. He tried moving his arm. It was stiff, as he had known it would be. The small brownish spots of blood that had seeped through the bandage reminded him of the ordeal he had experienced following the arrival of the doctor.

The doctor had gone about his business without delay. He had skillfully probed for the bullet and, after long minutes of excruciating pain which had caused Ki to grit his teeth to keep from crying out, he had found and removed it.

"Not too much damage done," he had said matter-of-factly as he applied antiseptic to the torn flesh of Ki's left shoulder and his patient endured the sting of the solution, which could not match the pain of the probing he had just endured. "There'll be a scar, but that's to be expected under the circumstances."

Ki had thanked and paid him, and when he had gone and Helen, after seeing the doctor out, had returned to the bedroom, he thanked her also but could not remember anything after that, for it was then that sleep quickly claimed him.

Later, as Helen returned carrying a tray on which rested a plate full of appetizing food and a cup of coffee, Ki sat up in the bed, bracing himself against a pillow he plumped up behind him, and proceeded to devour the food on the plate while a pleased Helen sat in a chair beside the bed and watched him, her hands folded placidly in her lap.

"It's been a long time—too long a time," he told her, "since I tasted such fine home cooking."

"I'm glad you're enjoying it."

"It's delicious."

"Would you like a second helping?" she asked when he had finished the meal.

He shook his head. "That was good and plenty."

Helen took the tray from him and placed it on the bedside table.

"Those two men—Dade and Rio—"

"I'm almost sorry I didn't shoot them," Helen said sharply. "I should have shot them. That would have taught them a lesson."

"I take it they were friends of Mike Brandon from the way they talked."

"I'm not so sure that's true. They've taken the side of the settlers in our dispute with the railroad, but I don't think Mike would claim them as friends."

"Oh? Why not?"

"They're not really on our side," Helen explained.

99

"All they really want is just a chance to raise Cain, never mind in the name of what cause. That doesn't matter to them. Mischief does. Which is typical of Texas trash like them. They shot a railroad agent and hurt him badly last week. That didn't set well with Mike. He's against that sort of thing. Which is why I said before that I don't think Mike considers that pair his friends. They can do our cause more harm than good in both the short and the long run, and Mike is well aware of that."

Helen paused and then, with an inquisitive glance at Ki, said, "I've been wondering about something."

"About what?"

"What did they mean when they said that you were bent on making trouble for us?"

"They were wrong. I'm not trying to make trouble for settlers like yourself. Your fight's not mine."

"You haven't answered my question."

"A friend of mine has been kidnapped, and I have reason to believe that the man who kidnapped her is Mike Brandon."

Helen's face bore an expression of shock followed by disbelief. "You think Mike Brandon—" She gave a strained little laugh. "Why, that's ridiculous! Mike a kidnapper? He'd never do a thing like that."

"Maybe he didn't, but, as I said, I have reason to believe he very well might have kidnapped my friend. That's why I've been asking questions about Brandon in town, which is what Dade and Rio meant when they said I was stirring up trouble."

"Why in the world would Mike Brandon want to kidnap your friend?" an incredulous Helen asked.

"My friend's name is Jessie Starbuck. She's a member of the Southern Pacific's board of directors. Whoever kidnapped her sent a note to the chairman of the board telling him that if he didn't change such railroad policies as the terminal rate and the evictions of the settlers occupying railroad land who won't or can't pay for the land they're living on, Jessie would be killed."

"Why, that's terrible!" Helen exclaimed. "Surely you can't seriously believe Mike Brandon would do such a terrible thing. Obviously, you don't know Mike, or you would never make such a charge. Mike is a kind and gentle man. He is a champion of the right and the just. He fights for the downtrodden even when he is fighting a losing battle.''

"Tell me something. Do you think the settlers' fight is a lost cause?''

Helen lowered her head. She nodded. "I've never said so to Mike or to my brother or to anyone else for that matter, but, yes, I do.'' Helen looked up at Ki. "I was planning to ask you why you had come to visit me. But now I don't think I need to ask you. I think I know why you came here. All this talk about kidnapping and Mike Brandon—you thought I might know where you could find Mike. That's true, isn't it?''

"Yes, it's true,'' Ki admitted, wishing he could deny it, wishing he had come to Helen's home simply to see her once more.

Helen rose. Folding her arms tightly across her chest, she walked to the window and looked out, her back to Ki. "Then it's also true that you are trying to make trouble for Mike and the rest of us who settled on railroad land, as Rio and Dade said you were.''

"I've already told you I'm not here to make trouble for you or any other settler,'' Ki insisted "I'm here to find my friend.''

"And you believe Mike Brandon has her.''

"Yes, I do. I came here to ask you if you could tell me where to find him.''

Helen's body stiffened as she stood silhouetted against the sunlight streaming through the window. "I could tell you where to find Mike. But I won't.''

"Helen, if Brandon has indeed kidnapped Jessie, as I firmly believe he has, he won't be doing himself or anybody else any good by holding or—hurting—her. Tell me where I can find him. I'll talk to him. I'm not looking for revenge for what he's done. I just want to stop him—if I'm not already too late—from doing her any harm. His kidnapping of Jessie was a foolish move, one that's bound to bring him trouble sooner or later. If you have

101

any friendly feeling for Brandon, tell me where he is so I can go there and stop him from doing something he'll live to regret for the rest of his life."

Helen nervously ran her hands up and down her upper arms.

She's going to tell me, Ki thought with suppressed excitement.

Helen suddenly turned to face Ki. With her head held high she said, "I won't tell you. I trust Mike. I know he wouldn't kidnap anybody. I would have known about it if he had. My brother is a good friend of Mike's, as am I. William would have told me if Mike had done what you say he's done." She stared at Ki, her expression stony, her eyes cold. "I don't think you should remain here any longer. You can only cause trouble for all of us. For all I know, you may even be an agent of the railroad who has come here to spread lies about Mike to discredit him and through him the settlers' struggle to protect their rights in the face of the railroad's arrogance and greed. I think you had better leave. Now."

Ki wanted to argue with her. He wanted to plead with her to tell him what he needed to know—the whereabouts of Mike Brandon. But it was obvious to him that she had no intention of giving that information to him. He had used up all his arguments and pleas. There was nothing for him to do now, he reasoned, but to leave as she wanted him to do. He reached for his shirt and pulled it on.

Not long afterward, when he was fully dressed, he left the soddy and Helen Simmons, freed his horse which he found tethered outside, swung into the saddle, and rode away as uninformed as when he had arrived. But he had no intention of giving up. I'll find her, he vowed. I just hope I find her before it's too late.

Jessie loosened her grip on the sycamore limb supporting her and then swung down to the ground. She stood there for a moment, listening. But she heard no sound of hooves hitting the ground, and she decided it was highly unlikely that the cattle that had long since disappeared from the area would turn and head back the way they had come to once again endanger her.

She shuddered at the memory. In her mind's eye she could see the cattle coming at her, the great horns on their heads swinging, their small eyes glittering in the flashes of lightning, their huge bodies a veritable avalanche of flesh that seemed intent on destroying her. She remembered a Starbuck cattle drive she had helped work a year ago and the stampede that had taken place during it that had killed one of her drovers. She remembered that when the stampede had ended, all anyone could find of the man who had gone down under the hooves of the stampeding steers was a broken and badly battered belt buckle. She shuddered again and surveyed the area.

No sign of Fowler's horse. Had it—She didn't want to consider the ugly possibility that the animal might not have escaped the stampede.

There's nothing for it, she thought, but to put shank's mare into action. She promptly did so. She walked west as the rain continued to fall but without the force it had had at the height of the storm. Now there was only an occasional angry rumble of thunder in the distance as the storm moved south. Lightning still flashed but on the horizon now.

She continued her trek, keeping an eye out for Fowler's bay. Some time later, when the rain had stopped and no thunder could be heard or lightning seen, she spotted the horse coming toward her from the west. She stopped in her tracks and stared in disbelief at it. Disbelief because now the horse was being led by a mounted man and that mounted man was Mike Brandon.

She turned and ran. The irony of her situation did not escape her as she fled. First she had run from stampeding steers. Now she was running from a kidnapping stud. She glanced over her shoulder. He was coming toward her at a leisurely trot, which indicated that he had complete confidence in his ability to run her down. She increased her pace, determined somehow to outwit if she couldn't outrun him. Another glance over her shoulder

103

revealed to her the infuriating fact that Brandon was smiling as he pursued her.

She had not gone another twenty yards before a loop of rope dropped out of the sky and around her body. It immediately tightened on her and went taut so that she could run no more.

As Brandon drew her toward him fighting every step of the way to free herself, his smile gave way to laughter. When he had reeled her in like a helpless fish on a line and she was standing beside him, he said, "You sure are a restless lady, aren't you? You can't seem to stay put in any one place for more than five minutes at a time. How did you manage to give Bill Fowler the slip?"

Jessie refused to answer as she began to remove Brandon's rope.

"Well, never mind. Bill'll tell me about it all in good time. You know, when I saw his horse wandering around all by his lonesome, I thought I was hunting for Bill. Only it turned out to be you I was after. Isn't this old world of ours just chock full of surprises, though?"

Still Jessie said nothing as she removed Brandon's rope.

"Now that we've run into each other again, Miss Starbuck, it occurs to me that I have something it might be good for you to see firsthand. You may remember I told Bill this morning that I was going calling on a fellow named Matt Cornell and his family, who were being evicted by your railroad. That's happening to them right this very minute, as a matter of fact." Brandon, as he began to gather up his rope, said, "You can get back aboard Bill's horse now."

Jessie hesitated. But if she didn't board the bay, she was sure Brandon would force her to walk to wherever it was he now intended to take her. She took the reins Brandon handed her and swung into the saddle.

"It's this way," he told her, beginning to retrace his route as he led the way west. "You should have stuck it out back there in the cabin with Bill," he suggested. "That way you wouldn't have gotten wet. Me, I rode out the storm inside Matt Cornell's house."

"I don't care where you spent your time, Mr. Brandon."

"Inside what *was* Matt Cornell's house," Brandon amended his previous remarks, ignoring Jessie's jibe.

Some time later he pointed to a one-story frame house painted white up ahead of them, which was situated in the midst of vast apricot groves. "That's the Cornell homestead."

They rode up to it and stopped beside a farm wagon that was piled high with household goods.

"Matt!" Brandon called out as he dismounted and indicated that Jessie was to do the same. "Matt Cornell!"

A tow-haired man in his twenties with sweat shining on his face emerged from the house. "Oh, it's you again, Michael. Did you forget something?"

"No, Matt, I ran into this lady on my way back to the cabin. She happens to be a member of the board of directors of the Southern Pacific line. I thought she might like the chance to hear from you and Meriah how things have been going with you lately."

"I've got nothing to say to the likes of her!" Cornell snarled and turned to reenter the house.

"Wait a minute, Matt," Brandon said. "Tell her what's happened here."

"She knows damn well what's happened here," Cornell said, turning to give Jessie a hate-filled glance.

"What is it, Matt?" asked a wan and worn-looking young woman who came out of the house at that moment. She raised a hand to shield her eyes from the sun that had come out. "Michael, this is a surprise. I thought we'd said our farewells."

Brandon introduced Jessie to the woman, who turned out to be Meriah Cornell, Matt's wife. "I brought Miss Starbuck here to learn firsthand about what her line's been doing to folks like us."

"It's been ruining us, that's what it's been doing," Cornell muttered, his eyes never leaving Jessie's face.

"If you're talking about the land, Mr. Cornell," Jessie said, "I've been given to understand that the railroad has offered to sell you the land and only if you refuse that offer does the issue become one of a legal eviction.''

''Well, I say you've been given to understand wrong, lady!'' Cornell snapped. ''We were promised a chance to buy land for a few dollars an acre when the line first talked us into coming and settling out here. Five dollars an acre tops.''

''I think there's been a misunderstanding,'' Jessie said. ''My understanding is that the original promise involved an offer of from two-fifty to five dollars per acre *and up*.''

''I suppose that's technically true,'' Cornell reluctantly admitted. ''But they said that *most* of the land would be sold at between two fifty and five dollars an acre. They upped the price sky-high on account of the improvements we made to the land. I'm talking homes we built and crops we put down like this house and those fruit trees of ours. That's not fair.''

A little girl wearing a blue calico dress and high-button black shoes, her hair in stiff pigtails, came out of the house, a forlorn expression on her face. ''Ma, I can't find my dolly.''

''Hush, Lizzie, I'm busy,'' Meriah Cornell told the child.

''I don't want to go to wherever we're going without I find my dolly,'' the child whimpered, on the verge of tears.

''Lizzie, you and me, we'll go find your dolly,'' Brandon volunteered. Taking the child by the hand, he started for the door of the house.

Jessie reached out and put her hand on the bay's saddle horn, waiting for the pair to disappear from sight, ready to flee.

At the door Brandon halted and turned back to face her. ''Don't try it, Miss Starbuck,'' he warned. ''You'll never make it. That's a promise.''

Damn you, Jessie thought. The man's a mind reader, she thought, only vaguely aware of the puzzled stares Matt and Meriah Cornell gave Brandon before he and Lizzie entered the house.

106

"I can't pay your line's price," Cornell told Jessie. "It takes time—years—to get groves like ours to the point where they're a profit-making proposition. Meanwhile, we're just about able to keep our heads above water one way or another. Where do you think we're going to get the thirty-five dollars per acre you want for this land you've taken title to? The bank in town won't give us another dime. I went and checked yesterday. Mr. Peters, he says fruit-growing's too risky a business for him to lend another dime to the likes of us.

"But we could have hung on if the railroad had given us credit. A chance to pay a little at a time as we went along. That seems to me the decent thing they could have done. But no. Not the Southern Pacific. They want cash on the barrelhead, and they got it for our land from some speculator from down in San Diego."

"That man gets our fruit trees, and it's him that will be harvesting our crop when the time comes," Meriah Cornell told Jessie. "Like my husband said, that's just not fair. Not one bit fair is it."

Jessie heard the bitterness in the woman's voice, which was tinged with despair.

"When you come right down to it," Cornell continued, "it's the railroad that's put us in this fix in more ways than one. You've gone and raised the terminal rate again. By a whopping eight percent this time around. It about done us in even before they got around to evicting us from our homeplace. I order goods from San Diego, say. The Southern Pacific doesn't drop them off in Groveland. No, sir, what they do is ship them all the way up to San Francisco and then they ship them back down from there to Groveland, which means I get soaked for freight charges both ways. That happens, too, when I ship fruit to my customers. Say I want to ship to my customers up in Spokane in southern Washington State. My fruit gets sent north to Seattle and then shipped back down south, and again I get hit with freight charges in both damned directions!

"But that's not even the worst of it. Since last year I've had railroad agents coming around here telling me

107

I have to open my books to them. If I don't, they say, they won't let me ship my fruit on the Southern Pacific. After they get a gander at my books, they adjust—how do you like that word: *adjust*—their rates for my fruit shipments so that I have to be the next best thing to an acrobat to make a profit however small and not fall head-first into bankruptcy.

"Your line, lady, it's trickier than any magician practicing his sleight of hand and greedier than a sow with a passel of new piglets to nurse."

"It's hard to keep a business like ours going that way, Miss Starbuck," Meriah Cornell said softly. "It does seem that the railroad means for hardworking folk like ourselves to have a real tough time of it while they get richer by the minute off of us. It wears a person down. I've been a fighter all my life, Miss Starbuck, but how can anyone fight that sort of system? How, I ask you? Well, I'm sorry to say I know the answer. Which is you can't fight them and win. You just can't, no matter how hard you might try. We fought along with Michael after the line evicted him from his homeplace, and this is all we have to show for our fighting. A wagonload of goods to take with us and our memories of all the dreams we had that died here to leave behind."

Meriah Cornell bit her lower lip and then covered her mouth with her hand to try to choke back her sobs. As tears flooded from her eyes, she turned and ran inside the house, almost colliding with Brandon, who, with Lizzie in his arms, was coming out of it.

"Mr. Cornell," Jessie said, "I think you raise valid points concerning the terminal rate, and they are ones I will investigate"—Jessie gave Brandon a baleful look—"just as soon as I am able to do so."

"Woman's tears," Cornell muttered angrily, gazing into the house at his weeping wife. "That's the legacy your line leaves people like us, Miss Starbuck. Woman's tears and men's curses."

"You've heard the settlers' side of the story now, I take it," Brandon said to Jessie. When she nodded, he said, "Then it's time we were going." He put Lizzie down on the ground and hunkered down in front of her. "I'll say good-bye to you again like I did when I was here before. You promise to be a good girl and don't make your ma or pa fret, okay?"

"I will, Mr. Brandon."

He kissed Lizzie on the cheek and straightened up.

"Thank you for finding me my dolly."

"Glad to do it, Lizzie. *Had* to do it. Why, you couldn't be expected to leave here without your dolly. Anybody with but half a brain in his head knows that."

Lizzie gave Brandon a smile of absolute adoration.

He gestured toward Jessie, and she climbed into the saddle of Fowler's bay. "Good-bye, Matt," he said, shaking hands with Cornell. "If I ever get up north, I'll be sure to stop by and see you all." A wink at Lizzie. "Including Dolly."

He received another worshipful smile from Lizzie.

Then Brandon was in the saddle and asking Cornell to say good-bye to Meriah for him.

"I didn't know you could be so understanding," Jessie remarked as they rode away together.

"Understanding?"

"The way you were with Lizzie. I remember very well that a lost dolly to a little girl is a tragedy of immense proportions. It was very nice of you to take her plight seriously and help her find her lost doll."

"I'm not as black a devil as some try to paint me, Miss Starbuck."

"Listening to Mr. and Mrs. Cornell, I realize clearly that they have been laboring under unusual difficulties. The matter of the evictions—I don't know what, if anything, I can do about them, but I do know that I will look into the matter of the way the line imposes—and continually increases—the terminal rate for shippers such as the Cornells."

Brandon let out a piercing whistle through his teeth. "Well, now, that's a surprise, that is."

"I'm not as black a devil as some try to paint me, Mr. Brandon."

"Tit for tat. Turnabout's fair play."

"I also question the right—certainly the propriety—of agents representing the Southern Pacific demanding access to the financial records of men like Mr. Cornell. That, too, is something that I think needs looking into." Jessie paused. Then, staring straight ahead and not at Brandon, she added, "Of course, I can do nothing to try to change things that might be wrong while I am being held prisoner by you."

"I could let you go," Brandon mused thoughtfully. "But what would happen if I do? Would you keep your word—"

"Mr. Brandon, I'll have you know that my word is my bond."

"Maybe you'd just forget all about the settlers around here and the problems they're having with your line. Then, too, maybe one person such as yourself would simply turn out to be a lone voice crying in the wilderness. Maybe there's no way in this wide world that you could effect any meaningful change that would help others before what happened to Matt and Meriah happens to them, too. No, I think a bird in the hand—pardon me. I think a member of the board of directors of the Southern Pacific Railroad in the hand is worth two in the bush up in San Francisco."

Despite herself, Jessie couldn't help smiling at his torturous reworking of the old saw. "I thought, the way you were just revising that saying, that you would surely have something to say about a chicken flying the coop."

"Well, you've done that twice already, haven't you? I never state the obvious, not if I can help it."

"Isn't it obvious to you by now, Mr. Brandon, that I am quite sincerely interested in and sympathetic to the settlers' struggle that has been taking place in this area?"

"Interested and sympathetic never righted any wrongs that I know of. That note I sent to your colleague, Mr. Benjamin Harrison, however—*it* just might get done what needs doing."

Later, as they approached a large group of men riding at right angles to their trail, Jessie recognized the rider in the lead as Isaac Pendleton, head of the local Grange

110

chapter, who had earlier visited Brandon at the cabin in the company of Bill Fowler.

At the same moment Pendleton raised his hand and waved. "Good day to you, Mike."

"Where you fellows headed?" Brandon asked as he and Jessie rode up to the group.

"We went by your place, Mike," Pendleton said. "Thought you'd want to come with us. We're on our way to make mischief for the railroad."

Brandon frowned. "What kind of mischief do you boys have it in mind to make?"

"We're going to derail a train," Pendleton replied.

"I wouldn't do that if I were you."

"You wouldn't? Why not?"

"For the simple reason that actions like that will discredit us and our cause. The railroad can use that sort of misadventure to tar and feather us in the newspapers as just a wild bunch of hooligans who don't deserve a fair hearing."

Before Pendleton could comment, one of the men with him said, "Mike, you're acting all too tame to suit a lot of us Grangers. We think it's time somebody raised a little hell with the line to make them understand we mean business."

"Don't you fellows think I meant business when I kidnapped Jessica Starbuck here?" Brandon quickly countered.

"Sure, you did," the same man admitted. "But what good did it get us, you and your kidnapping? Everything's the same as it was before you brought her here. Which is why we've decided it's our turn to do something that will make the bosses sit up and take notice of us."

"That's exactly my point, Joe," Brandon said. "The railroad'll sit up and take notice of us all right if you do what you say you're going to do. But it won't be the kind of notice we want or can benefit from."

"Mike," Pendleton said, "Joe's got a point. I agree with him. The fact of the matter is that your kidnapping of Miss Starbuck hasn't gotten us anywhere. Things remain exactly as they were before you brought her here, which leads a lot of us to think that Ben Harrison and his cohorts don't give a tinker's damn about what happens or doesn't happen to Jessica Starbuck.''

A chill coursed through Jessie at Pendleton's harsh words, because deep within herself she knew that what the man had just said might very well be true.

"Kidnapping her's not enough, it begins to look like,'' Joe declared, eliciting murmurs of agreement from the assembled men. "Maybe the time's come to make good on your threat to kill her if the railroad won't give in to us. Have you thought about that, Mike?''

Brandon's face was impassive but a muscle in his jaw jumped. "What I've thought about is how hotheads like you, Joe, can be the ruin of all I've worked and fought so hard for.''

"I don't see any results of your working and your fighting,'' Joe said in a surly voice, and many of the men with him nodded their agreement.

Turning to their leader, Brandon said, "Isaac, instead of derailing the train, which could injure and maybe even kill people, why not just pile logs and such on the track to stop it? That way nobody would get hurt.''

"You know I'm not a violent man, Mike,'' Pendleton said. "But these men—''

"I'm not talking to these men now, Isaac, I'm talking to the man who leads them and is, I believe, strong enough to control them.''

Pendleton's troubled eyes were on Brandon's face. They never wavered. Nor did his voice when he said, "Mike's right, men. We're not out to do harm to anyone. We'll block the tracks and let it go at that.'' When mutterings of discontent and disapproval greeted his statement, he added, "For now.''

Brandon turned his horse and rode away with Jessie at his side.

"I think you did the sensible thing back there,'' Jessie told him a few minutes later.

"It's getting to be that I have to try my damnedest to keep a lid on a pot that's about to boil over any minute,''

112

he said, talking more to himself than to Jessie. "Things can't go on like this much longer."

The words were no sooner out of his mouth than a shot rang out and Brandon pitched forward in his saddle, hitting his horse's neck and almost causing the animal to bolt.

Jessie looked over her shoulder and saw the figure of the man who had fired the shot silhouetted on a ridge behind them, the sunlight glinting on the barrel of his rifle. As he raised the weapon to his shoulder and took aim, she grabbed Brandon's reins and looped them over the head of his horse.

"Hang on!" she yelled. Leading Brandon's horse, she went galloping away from the spot.

Another shot sounded but went wild.

When they were safely out of range of the gunman, Jessie tightened her grip on her reins, and the bay slowed. "You all right?" she asked Brandon, who was clinging to his saddle horn, his head bent.

He managed a nod.

"Which way to the cabin?"

Brandon pointed and gave Jessie directions. By the time they reached the cabin, he was bleeding profusely.

Jessie sprang from the saddle and proceeded to help him dismount. As she was doing so, Fowler came out of the cabin and said, "Hey, Mike, you caught her! Good for you! That hellcat darn near brained me when she made her getaway." Then, seeing the blood on Brandon's back, he asked, "What the hell happened?"

"Help me get him inside," Jessie said, and Fowler did so.

After laying the wounded man facedown on a bed, Fowler repeated his question.

"Somebody shot him," Jessie answered. "The bullet's still in his back. Boil some water and get me some clean cloths. Antiseptic, if you have it."

"The closest thing around here to antiseptic is whiskey."

"Get it, along with the other things. Hurry!"

As Fowler was heating water on the stove, he said to Jessie, "I take it Mike caught up with you."

"She ran right into my arms," a weak Brandon murmured in a barely audible voice. "I always told you, Bill; that I was irresistible to women."

"I wish I was," Fowler said with a weak laugh. "If I was, maybe she wouldn't have hit me with that stool over there when she got away from me."

Jessie proceeded to strip Brandon's shirt from him, and then, when Fowler brought her a basin full of hot water, she bathed the wound, gently examining the shattered flesh around the small bullet hole in Brandon's body. "I need a knife."

"Take mine."

She took the pocket knife Fowler handed her and said, "This is going to hurt, Mike."

He turned his head toward her. "Nice to hear my name on your pretty lips. Can I call you Jessica?"

"Try Jessie. Are you ready?"

"Go ahead and do it," Brandon said stoically.

As Jessie began to probe for the bullet, Brandon gritted his teeth and squeezed his eyes shut. As she continued working on him, he groaned and then stifled a cry as the blade of the knife in her hand dug deep into his flesh.

"I've found it," Jessie breathed and bent closer to see the wound better. The knife in her hand glinted as it brought the bullet out.

Brandon's body went limp. He opened his mouth and sucked in air. The sweat on his face dampened the pillow under his head.

Jessie picked up the whiskey bottle Fowler had brought her and poured some of its contents onto a cloth, which she used to wipe the wound clean.

"What are you doing to him?" Fowler asked anxiously as she squeezed the ragged flesh around the mouth of the wound.

"Making it bleed," she answered curtly. "That's the best thing to do to avoid infection when you're working without an antiseptic." Moments later she wiped away the excess blood with a damp cloth and applied more whiskey to the wound. Then, after tearing the cloth Fowler had given her into bandages, she proceeded to dress Brandon's wound.

Like him, she was sweating when she finished her task.

Fowler picked up the basin of bloody water and the equally bloody cloth and carried them out of the cabin.

Brandon gazed up at Jessie. "You could have—when I was shot—you could have escaped."

She said nothing.

"Why didn't you?"

"You mean why didn't I run off and leave behind such an irresistible-to-women man as yourself to make it on your own? I should think the answer would be obvious to you."

"I wish there was truth—a little bit of truth, anyway— behind your teasing," Brandon whispered plaintively.

Jessie suspected that there was but didn't say so. She was far too confused by the puzzle her own recent actions had presented to her. Why hadn't she tried to escape from Brandon following the shooting? She could have done so easily. He wouldn't have been able to trail her, not shot the way he was. But here she was tending to the wound of the man who had kidnapped her.

"That backshooter almost succeeded in doing what he set out to do, which was to kill me," a weary Brandon murmured. "Maybe it was one of the hotheads riding with Isaac Pendleton."

Jessie hesitated a moment and then said softly, "Maybe the man with the gun wasn't shooting at you at all. Have you stopped to think that he might have been shooting at me?"

★

Chapter 7

Ki left the Groveland Hotel early the next morning after a long, mostly sleepless, night. The little sleep he did get had been haunted by a series of brief but alarming dreams in which Jessie appeared, always in peril, with him unable, for one reason or another, to help her.

Now, as he crossed the street, he had to force himself to pay attention to his surroundings instead of to the fear he was feeling concerning Jessie's possible plight, or he would run the risk of being run down by a wagon or some other equally disastrous experience.

The town of Groveland was up early and already about its business. The streets were filled with wagons and men on horseback. The stores as filled with shoppers. On the corner a fruit merchant hawked his wares at the top of his lungs, his voice loud but competing unsuccessfully with a competitor for the attention of passersby on the opposite corner who had a tray full of gilded shaving mugs for sale.

Ki made his way to the nearest restaurant, not really

wanting to eat but feeling he had to do so to keep up his strength if for no other reason.

Where was Jessie?

The question echoed in his mind.

So did another one: *Was she all right?*

Both questions tormented him as he entered the restaurant and sat down at the first empty table he came to. He cursed himself for his failure to find her. He damned himself for not having solved the mystery of her disappearance. He deeply regretted the unwillingness of people to talk to him, to tell him what he so desperately needed to know. The latter element that was upsetting him bore grim testimony, he thought, to the seeds the Southern Pacific's management had sown and which had led directly to the angry harvest of silence he was now reaping in his search for the person he cared most for in the whole world, more even than he cared for himself.

"May I help you, sir?"

The waitress who had spoken to Ki was young and not very pretty, but she had bright eyes and an attractive smile. She stood with pencil poised over a little pad, her eyes on her customer.

"A soft-boiled egg, please," Ki said. "Tea."

"That's all, sir?"

Ki nodded and the waitress left him alone.

He sat there at the table, drumming his fingers upon it as he stared through the window at the people passing by outside without really seeing them. What he saw instead was a vision of Jessie, luminous in the early morning sunlight and radiant in her natural beauty as she gazed longingly at him.

He resisted the urge to rise and leave the restaurant to continue his search for her. He forced himself to remain where he was, and a few minutes later, when the waitress returned with his order, he proceeded to crack the shell of the brown egg in its china cup and begin to spoon its contents into his mouth.

Tasteless.

He took a sip of steaming tea. It soothed him slightly. But then he put down his spoon, unable to finish eating his egg, his stomach like lead within him. He drank some more tea.

What next? he asked himself. Where do I go? Whom do I try to get to talk to me? He didn't know the answers to his questions. A feeling of frustration welled up in him, and in its wake came anger at the feeling of helplessness that was almost overwhelming.

The sound of laughter drifted through the open door of the restaurant from the street. So did the jingle of harness chains. The sounds of ordinary everyday life. Its sights, too. Women passing. Women he, at any other time, would have found of interest. But not today. Today he saw only—

His eyes narrowed. Was that—

It was. He watched the woman seated beside the man in the wagon that was pulling up across the street in front of the General Store. The woman who was Helen Simmons. The man with her—she had said she lived with her brother. Was that her brother with her now?

Both of them went into the store.

Was Helen Simmons the answer to the questions he had been asking himself a moment ago? Should he try once more to persuade her to tell him what she obviously knew about the whereabouts of Mike Brandon?

He drank some more tea, its steam curling up around his face as he kept his eyes on the door of the store across the street. He knew it was a slim chance that she would even speak to him after their unpleasant parting earlier, let alone tell him what he so needed to know. But who else could he talk to who would be willing to help him? No one. At least, no one that he knew of who knew what Helen knew about Brandon. And, if she refused to talk to him, perhaps the man with her, the man who might be her brother, would tell him what she wouldn't.

He beckoned to the waitress, paid his bill, and was waiting beside the wagon when Helen and her male companion emerged from the General Store a little while later.

When Helen saw him, she stopped in her tracks, the smile that had been on her face fading fast. Then, recovering her composure, she walked on and placed the several boxes she was carrying in the bed of the wagon.

"It's the railroad that's to blame," said the man with her as he placed a crate, which was filled with boxes and sacks of various sizes, in the wagon bed. "Imagine. Forty-seven cents for a pound of cornmeal. I bet a good third of that forty-seven cents is charged by the store to make up the freight charges levied on them to get the cornmeal here on the train."

"Good morning, Helen," Ki said as she was about to climb into the wagon's seat.

"Good morning." Her voice was cold, her expression severe.

"Let me give you a hand in climbing up there," Ki offered.

"Thank you, but I can manage quite well on my own."

The man with Helen climbed into the driver's seat, and she climbed up beside him.

"Helen, I want to talk to you if you'll spare me a few minutes," Ki said.

"I have nothing further to say to you."

"Well, I have a lot I want to say to you."

"A friend of yours, Helen?" inquired the man seated next to her.

"An acquaintance," she replied. "His name is Ki. Ki, this is my brother, William Fowler."

The man stared with evident hostility at Ki, who was staring back at him steadily, the name William Fowler triggering memories for Ki. Both Jessie and Benjamin Harrison had told him, he now recalled, that a man named Bill Fowler was Mike Brandon's right-hand man.

"If Mr. Fowler is your brother, Helen," Ki said, his eyes still on Fowler, "how come his last name's different from yours?"

"William is my half-brother, if that's any business of yours. Our father married twice. William, shall we go?"

"You have some business with my sister?" Fowler asked Ki.

"In a manner of speaking, yes, I do. Your sister was

120

good enough to help me out when I ran into some gun-trouble the other day.''

"She told me about that," Fowler said. "Maybe that gun-trouble, as you call it, will teach you to keep your nose out of other people's business from now on. I've heard tell of you, Ki. If you want some sound advice, I'd say you ought to leave town before somebody doesn't just shoot you but winds up killing you.''

"I heard from a friend of mine, a Miss Jessica Starbuck, about how you and Mike Brandon caused a ruckus at the Southern Pacific's stockholders' meeting in San Francisco recently," Ki said calmly. "I also heard from Ben Harrison that you're a close confederate of Mike Brandon's. Did you lend him a hand in the kidnapping of Miss Starbuck?''

"How dare you say such a thing!" an irate Helen exclaimed, her eyes flashing fire. "First you accuse Mike of kidnapping your lady friend, and now you have the nerve to accuse my brother of the same thing. William, drive on.''

But Fowler didn't. Instead he told Ki, "I've got nothing to say to the likes of you. Except one last thing. Leave town and let us be. Our affairs aren't any business of yours.''

"You're mistaken about that," Ki said. "When it comes to you and Brandon kidnapping my good friend, Miss Starbuck, your affairs turn out to be definitely my business as well.''

Before Fowler could say anything more, Ki continued, "Where have you got her?''

"I don't know what you're talking about. The last time I saw Jessica Starbuck was in San Francisco at the stockholders' meeting.''

"If you aren't mixed up in this nasty business," Ki said, "then maybe you'll be willing to tell me where I can find Mike Brandon.''

"If you want Mike, you'll have to find him for yourself," Fowler snapped. "You'll get no help from me.''

"Nor will you get any help from me," Helen added as her brother released the brake and drove the farm wagon out into the middle of the street, leaving Ki to stand and stare at the departing conveyance.

But he didn't stand and stare for long. Before the wagon was out of sight, he turned and sprinted down the street to the livery barn to get his horse, which he had left there the night before following his return to Groveland from Helen Simmons's house.

As Jessie awoke, the ropes that bound both of her hands to the metal frame of the bed on which she had been sleeping bit into her wrists.

She lay there in the light of early morning, fuming about the fact that after what she had done for Brandon—removing the bullet from his back and then cleansing and bandaging his wound, he had ordered Fowler to tie her hands—both of them this time—to the bed frame. That order had followed Fowler's announcement that he needed to go home to help his sister with the work that needed doing at their homestead.

After Fowler had carried out Brandon's order, he left them alone, promising to return as soon as he could.

But Fowler had not returned, at least, not yet. Jessie glanced longingly at the stool that had served her as a weapon not very long ago. Then she glanced at the sleeping form of Brandon lying on a bed across the room. He was still shirtless, his upper torso covered only by the bandage she had placed on his back. He lay with his face turned toward her, his eyes closed, his right arm hanging down toward the floor.

She strained at her bonds but could not break them. The bedsprings creaked as a result of her efforts. The sound was loud enough to awaken Brandon, who sat up with a groan and stared suspiciously at her.

The naked upper half of his body glowed golden in the sunlight coming through the window as he sat there facing her.

Jessie forced herself to look away from him. But when she heard his footsteps coming toward her, she looked back at him. He was standing a few feet away from her. He towered over her.

"These ropes are too tight," she said stonily. "They hurt."

"If I took them off, you'd be out that door so fast it would, I wager, make my head swim."

She couldn't promise him that she wouldn't do the very thing he had said she would do, so she said nothing more. She wouldn't—she *would not*—plead with him for anything, not for release from her uncomfortable and potentially precarious predicament or for anything else for that matter. Such as food to satisfy her growing hunger. She had pleaded with him once when she had asked him to let her go and present his side of the story to the other members of the railroad's board of directors, but her pleas had only made him angry and gained her nothing. She would not, she vowed now, make the same humiliating mistake twice.

"I dreamed of you last night," he said in a low voice, still towering over her and still staring down at her. "It was a most arousing dream."

She tried to look away from him, but his eyes held her.

"If things had been different—if we had met under different circumstances—" He made a gesture of helplessness with both hands, and Jessie thought he sighed softly, but she wasn't sure.

Her anger toward him returned. "The very least you could do is loosen these ropes, if not set me free. Tieing me up like this is wrong in light of what I did for you yesterday."

"Wrong, maybe," he admitted. And then added, "But necessary."

"If I were going to escape, I could have done it when whoever it was shot you on our way back here. Doesn't that tell you something about me?"

"It tells me that you were unwilling to abandon me when I was hurt so badly. But your two attempts to escape also tell me something about you. Namely, that you'll try to escape again the first chance you get now that you know I'm going to remain among the living awhile longer and I'm not in need of you."

123

Before she could say anything, he repeated his last words. "I'm not in need of you." He gave a self-mocking laugh. "Good Lord, what a lie that is! I *am* in need of you, Jessie. In *desperate* need of you, and I think you know that."

She knew nothing of the kind. His words surprised her. Weren't they enemies? What need did enemies have for each other? Except to hate, to injure, to try to kill each other? But the light she saw being kindled in Brandon's eyes as he continued staring down at her was not born of hate. On the contrary. It was born of desire. She couldn't help wondering if the same wild light was alive in her own green eyes as she returned his penetrating stare.

He moved closer to her and placed one knee on the bed. He reached out and touched her cheek with his hand. It was a gentle touch that soon turned passionate as he bent his head and kissed her on the lips. She tried to turn her head away from him but was unable to do so. A voice within her silently whispered: "*Unable to do so or unwilling to do so?*"

She began to return his kiss. She fought the ropes that bound her wrists to the bed, wanting to be able to embrace him as he lay down beside her and his hand caressed her breasts and then began to lift her dress.

"Don't," she said as his lips left hers, but he didn't stop.

Moments later, as he undid his trousers and then began to finger her, she didn't want him to stop. She was defeated, she realized, by her own desire that matched his own. She was aware of the wetness on her thighs that had been left there by her own juices, and she realized that her own emotions and her own body, subject to them, had not only revealed her desire for him but had also betrayed her spoken order to him to not do what he was now so eagerly doing.

As his hand cupped her moist mound, he inserted his middle finger deep within her, where it twisted and turned in its hot explorations. She felt his erection throbbing against her thigh and wanted it, not his finger. Wanted it more than anything else in the world at that passionate moment. As he withdrew his finger and rolled over on top of her, she cried out in sensual delight when his shaft began to plow the path his finger had previously taken.

He groaned with pleasure and arched his back. Slowly he began to move upon her. He kissed her neck, her forehead, her lips. He increased the tempo of his movements, rising and falling upon her in a rhythm that again made her cry out and throw back her head. As she writhed with pleasure beneath him, he raised himself on his hands so that he could look down at her face, where a series of emotions were being mirrored.

Watching her closely, he brought her to the brink of a climax and then, with deft movements, eased her back down from the peak she had almost reached.

"Do it!" she heard herself order him. *"Oh, do it now. Please!"*

He did it, maddening her with ecstasy as she climaxed.

But it was not over. With barely a pause, he continued plunging into her almost violently, and she, abandoning herself to her feelings of fleshly desire, began to shudder so violently that the bed shook and its springs screamed. The second time she came, a few minutes later, she gave a series of little grunts, her head tossing from side to side.

He dropped down upon her. His hips began to pound her, and she reveled in the pounding. A moment later she felt him flood her, felt his body shudder in a series of spasms as hers had just done, and rejoiced in the intense pleasure she had been able to give him.

Then, with all of it over and ended, they both slowly returned to reality. Jessie, to anger at him, Brandon to regretful awareness of the broad gulf that separated them and made a mockery of the delight they were each able to give to the other.

"I wish we could do business as satisfactorily as we make love," Jessie murmured as she lay relaxed and unmoving on the bed beside Brandon.

He grunted something unintelligible, his face half-buried in the pillow.

"Really, I do. Why won't you listen to reason?"

"Because the railroad won't."

"That's a ridiculous position to take."

Brandon raised his head. "Ridiculous, is it? I suppose I should expect something like that from you. Anything that doesn't fit in with what you want on behalf of your precious railroad is 'ridiculous.' Well, I'm here to tell you you're wrong and it's not, not by a damn sight." Brandon began to dress.

"Untie me."

"No."

"I have to get dressed. I can't just lie here like this. I imagine I look like a doll somebody got tired of playing with and left in this sorry state." Jessie immediately regretted her words because her analogy had hit too close to home in light of what she and Brandon had just done.

He glanced at her. "You won't try anything?"

I damned well will if I get half a chance, she thought. But she said, "You can stand right there and watch my every move."

He did just that after he had untied her hands. He stood beside the bed watching as she adjusted her clothes and ran her fingers through her badly tousled hair.

His response to her languid and, apparently to him, erotic movements was evident in the thickening length of flesh bulging beneath the cloth of his trousers.

"You want some breakfast?" he asked huskily when she had finished arranging her clothes.

"Yes. If it's not too much trouble."

He started to reach for the ropes lying on the bed beside Jessie which had bound her hands. But his hand halted halfway to them, and he turned swiftly at the sound of a horse's hoofbeats coming from outside the cabin. He went to the window.

"It's Fowler," he said, more to himself than to Jessie. "He's back like he said he would be."

Brandon left the window and went to the wooden cupboard near the stove. He was opening it when the door burst open and Fowler came into the room, slamming the door behind him.

126

"What's the big hurry?" Brandon asked him. "You look like you've been riding hard. Anything wrong?"

"Damn right something's wrong. Her friend is what's wrong. I was in town with Helen getting our weekly order from the General Store, and he showed up. I told you, Mike, when Isaac Pendleton and I came here before that fellow named Ki was in town asking people where he could find you."

"I remember. Is that what he asked you?"

"Not exactly. What he asked me was did I have a hand in helping you kidnap her." He gestured toward Jessie.

Brandon took down a sack of flour from the cupboard. "He knows I kidnapped her?" he asked incredulously.

"I don't think he *knows*. But he sure as shooting strongly suspects you did. That's evidently why he's been trying to run you down. But up till now, so far as I know, he never accused you of kidnapping."

"How does he happen to know about me?"

"He said she told him about us being at the stockholders' meeting in San Francisco. He also said Ben Harrison said I was your right-hand man. I reckon he's just gone and put two and two together—"

"And come up with four," Brandon interrupted grimly. He was about to say more when the door burst open again and struck Fowler, who had been standing just inside it, and nearly knocked him down.

"Ki!" Jessie cried as her friend, a five-pointed *shuriken* in each hand entered the room.

"Watch!" Ki ordered both men after glancing at Jessie to assure himself that she was all right. Without a moment's hesitation he threw the *shuriken* in his left hand, and it embedded itself up to its pintle point in the door of the cupboard. "This one," he said, holding up the five-pointed metal throwing star in his right hand, "will just as easily bury itself in a man's body or brain the way that one ate its way into wood. So don't either of you make a move. I don't want to hurt you fellows, but I'll tell you this. I will hurt you and hurt you bad if you do anything to stop Jessie and me from leaving."

127

"Jesus Christ crucified!" Fowler exclaimed as he stared in awe at the *shuriken* protruding from the cupboard's wooden door. "One of those things could put a man's lights out once and for all."

"He's right," Ki said coldly to Brandon.

"How'd you find me?" Brandon asked as Jessie got up from the bed and crossed the room to stand beside Ki.

"I had a little chat in town with your friend, Fowler," Ki answered. "Then, when he and his sister took off in their wagon, I got my horse from the livery barn and followed them to their soddy. I stayed out of sight, and then, when Fowler got his saddle horse and rode out, I followed him. He led me straight here, I'm happy to say."

"We didn't hurt her," Brandon said, mesmerized by the steely glint in Ki's eyes.

"It's a good thing you didn't," Ki told him. "If you had, you'd be dead by now."

Almost before the sound of Ki's last word had faded away, Brandon hurled the sack of flour in his hand.

Ki shoved Jessie to one side and nimbly stepped out of the way of the missile before it could strike either of them.

But it did strike the jamb of the open door behind them, and as it did so clouds of white flour flew up into the air.

Jessie, inhaling some of the cabin's flour-polluted air, began to cough.

Ki, breathing shallowly, to inhale as little air as possible, seized her by the arm and shoved her outside.

Brandon chose that moment to lunge forward and seize him by the shoulders. At the same time he shouted, "Get her, Fowl—"

Ki's swift left-handed chop to the right side of Brandon's neck cut off the man's speech and sent him reeling across the room. Pocketing the *shuriken* he still had in his right hand, Ki went after Brandon.

At the same time Jessie managed to fend off Fowler, who was attempting to seize her. Her right leg shot up

128

and gave the man attempting to prevent her from getting away an explosive kick in the center of the chest, a kick Ki had taught her. Fowler gasped as the air shot from his lungs, leaving him barely able to breathe.

A straight-hand chop, similar to the one Ki had just given Brandon, dropped Fowler to the floor, where he lay without moving, his eyes open but totally sightless.

Jessie moved in to help Ki, who was grappling with Brandon, but she quickly found that her help was unneeded.

Ki seized Brandon's right wrist. Turning his back to his opponent, he bent at the waist and pulled. Brandon went flying over Ki's head to hit the table, smashing it to pieces, and land on the floor amid the splintered wood. He lay there groggily, trying but failing to get his feet under him.

"Let's get out of here," Ki said, taking Jessie by the hand.

They ran outside, where they both boarded Ki's black. Neither of them looked back as they went galloping away from the cabin and the two men it contained.

When they arrived in Groveland, Ki directed Jessie to the livery barn. There he returned the black he had rented and paid the farrier what he owed. Once outside again, he said, "We'd better get out of here as fast as we can. Let's find out how soon we can get a train to San Francisco."

As they made their way to the train station, Jessie said, "I don't think I was ever so glad to see anybody in my entire life as I was to see you back there at the cabin."

"You're sure you're all right?"

"I'm fine. Fit as a fiddle. Brandon treated me well enough." She smiled secretly to herself as she remembered the two times they had coupled and how well he had treated her each of those times. "So did Fowler. I don't really think they ever really intended to do me any harm."

"Maybe not. But I'm glad we got you out of their hands all the same. "

129

"*You* got me out of their hands, for which I'm most grateful."

They arrived at the train station and found that there was a northbound train due to arrive in Groveland within the hour. They bought tickets and waited on the nearly deserted platform, the minutes passing much too slowly to suit either of them.

Ki kept both eyes peeled for any sign of Brandon or Fowler, but neither man had put in an appearance by the time the train pulled into the station, and Ki and Jessie hurriedly boarded it. They took an empty seat in one of the coaches, and as she sat down beside Ki, Jessie permitted herself a heartfelt sigh.

"It's over," Ki said, lightly touching her hand.

"No, it's not."

He gave her a quizzical glance.

Responding to it, she explained, "When we get to San Francisco, I intend to go directly to Ben Harrison and tell him that I think it's high time certain policies of the Southern Pacific, which have been in place for some time—with my endorsement, as well as the endorsements of the other board members, I admit—were changed. We can make those changes in a special meeting of the board, which I want Ben to call."

"What policies are you talking about?"

"Let me tell you about a family I met who were being evicted. Their names were Matt and Meriah Cornell, and they had a small daughter named Lizzie."

Jessie talked at length about the evictions of families like the Cornells, the terminal rate and the damage it was doing to farmers and others, and about the shooting of Amos Copeland by Ben Harrison's chief of security, Chet Langley, when Copeland's wife tried to fight the eviction being carried out by Langley and the gunmen he had brought with him. By the time Jessie had finished speaking, she was feeling a righteous anger rising up within her, and Ki was fully informed about railroad policies that he, like Jessie, believed to be wrong and, in cases like that of the Copelands versus Chet Langley and his hired guns, criminal.

130

"You might run into some problems getting done what you want done, Jessie," Ki cautioned when she finished speaking.

"Oh, I expect there will be some opposition to some of my proposals among the members of the board," Jessie said, "but once I have a chance to explain what I've learned in the valley and seen there as well, I'm sure they will agree with me that change is not only necessary but imperative at this point."

Ki hesitated. He wasn't sure whether he should bring up the matter that was on his mind. On the other hand he felt it was incumbent upon him to tell Jessie about his conversation with Ben Harrison that had taken place on the day he had discovered Jessie missing. He decided to speak up.

"I went to see Harrison the day I found out you were missing," he began. "He didn't strike me as someone who would be easily persuaded to do anything very much different in the management of the Southern Pacific than what he has been doing all along. When I asked him why anybody might want to kidnap you—by the way, when I gave him the description of the man the hotel desk clerk had seen you with the night before, he said he thought it sounded like Brandon, which is why I went looking for him. But to get back to my point, when I asked Harrison why anyone would want to kidnap you, he began talking to me about the railroad's terminal rate and the price the line's appraiser had set on the settlers' acreage and so on. I told him I knew nothing about that sort of thing, but I assumed he wanted what I wanted, which was your safe return. He said he did, and I had no reason to doubt him. But he also said he wasn't about to give in to the demands of any kidnappers. He insisted that he would be remiss in his duties to the company and its stockholders if he did so."

Jessie frowned. "Perhaps Ben didn't appreciate the seriousness of the situation," she suggested.

"I don't like saying this, but I think he did indeed appreciate the seriousness of the situation. He just couldn't seem to lose sight of the railroad's needs, which,

131

it struck me, he was giving a higher priority to than he was to the danger you were facing.''

"Well, I'll explain things to Ben when I see him. I'm sure he'll listen to reason once he has all the facts at his disposal.''

Ki wasn't so sure, and that uncertainty bred a growing uneasiness within him. But he said nothing to Jessie about his feelings as the train sped along its tracks, heading for the city of San Francisco.

★

Chapter 8

"Jessie!" a surprised Benjamin Harrison exclaimed as she walked into his San Francisco office with Ki by her side. "Oh, my dear, I can't tell you how happy I am to see you!" He spread his arms wide, hurried to Jessie, and embraced her. Then, holding her out at arm's length, he asked, "Where were you? Why did you disappear so suddenly? What happened? Was it—"

"I'll tell you everything, Ben," she said as she and Ki sat down in chairs facing Harrison's desk and the board chairman sat down behind the desk. "To begin at the beginning, I was kidnapped by Mike Brandon."

"Then it was just as I told Ki I suspected all along!" Harrison exclaimed. Turning to Ki, and shaking a finger at him, he added, "Didn't I tell you Brandon would turn out to be the villain of the piece when we talked before you went searching for Jessie? Didn't I?"

"Yes, Mr. Harrison, you did," Ki responded.

"Excuse me, Jessie," Harrison said then, "I didn't mean to interrupt you. It's just that the very mention of Brandon's name makes my blood boil. Go on, please."

Jessie did.

"And you say you escaped twice from Brandon's clutches?" an amazed Harrison exclaimed.

"But it was the third time that was the charm, as they say," Jessie said self-deprecatingly. "Or I should say Ki was the charm. If it hadn't been for him, I would probably still be a prisoner in that cabin."

"I am so heartily glad you're not," Harrison said. "Now, then. During your account of your terrible ordeal, you mentioned some problems that you thought we should discuss. What problems did you have in mind, Jessie?"

"The way we have been handling the sales of the land we've taken title to in Fresno County. Many—most, I should say—of the settlers there are convinced that the price our appraiser has set on the land they've been working for many years is much too high—"

"Hold on a moment. Stop right there." Harrison, holding up a hand, continued, "We've been over and over this ground many times until I, for one, am weary of it. We've set what I consider to be a fair price for the acreage, and we have given the settlers the right of first refusal where the purchase of said land is concerned."

"The settlers feel we are including the value of the improvements they have made on the land in the price-per-acre we've put upon it. They argue that they took raw land and improved it with homesteads, farms, and as Mike Brandon mentioned to me during one of our discussions of this matter, even irrigation systems to make the land fertile. They feel that such things should not be factored into the per-acre price."

Harrison was becoming red in the face. He took a deep breath and leaned back in his chair. He folded his hands across his ample girth and said in a reasonable tone, "Jessie, you and I both know that the land in question is worth the price we've appraised it at in its present state. Its *present* state," he repeated for emphasis. "There are many men who would jump at the chance, and indeed have jumped, to obtain such valuable land."

"Speculators, by and large," Jessie interjected, "who are buying it for resale."

Harrison shrugged.

"Why don't we consider lowering the price we're asking for the land, Ben?"

"Why don't we—! Surely you can't be serious, Jessie."

"I'm completely serious. What harm would it do? We obtained the land at no cost from the federal government. There's no need for us to make a substantial profit on it at this point for that reason alone, not to mention the ill will it's causing and the bad publicity we're getting in the matter."

"I'll tell you what harm it would do!" Harrison suddenly thundered. "It would make us look like fools in front of our shareholders, who want us to make as large a profit as we can in the operation of the Southern Pacific and never mind how that profit is made. Do you want to let down the men and women who have invested not only their money but also their faith and trust in us?"

"Ben, I don't think this is a matter that can be put on a purely business basis. We have to consider our company's reputation among the people of this country. Our company's moral reputation, if you will."

"Well, I won't!"

Jessie ignored Harrison's outburst. "If we asked less for the land—say, what we originally promised to charge, which was two-fifty to five dollars an acre—"

"Our agreement stated that *most*, not *all*, of the acreage would sell in that price range."

Jessie decided to try the last argument she could muster to bolster her position. "Ben, that agreement to which you refer also stated the price of the land would be set without regard to improvements, and yet a few minutes ago you baldly stated that the appraiser did indeed take into consideration the improvements the settlers have made on that land when he set the land's sale price. I believe you spoke of the land's 'present state.' Now, that, in my book, is a blatant violation of the original agreement and a stain on the integrity of all of us. I strongly urge that we remove that stain by reducing the price substantially and promptly.''

"Jessie, Jessie, Jessie," Harrison crooned indulgently as if he were talking to a stubborn child. "It grieves me to hear you espousing the cause and position of our enemies in this matter. The position held by such rabble-rousers as Mike Brandon. I am at a complete loss to understand why you are doing this. Why you cannot or will not see that you are throwing your lot in with those who would ruin the line, bring it down as a pack of hounds brings down a fox in the heat of the hunt.''

"I am taking this position, Ben," Jessie said in a chilly tone as she tried to control her growing anger with the board chairman, "because I think it is the right one to take. Not to mention the fact that in the long run it is for the good of the Southern Pacific. As lowering the terminal rate would be."

An aghast Harrison could only stare at her as she proceeded to describe what she called "a terminal rate that borders on extortion" and pleaded for a rollback of the company's latest increase and a total restructuring of the manner in which the Southern Pacific determined its shipping terminals.

"Jessie, you know that a large percentage of the line's profits derive from what we charge to ship freight. To reduce those charges would mean to reduce our overall net profit, and that, at least to me, is unthinkable. I, for one, will not agree to a rollback of rates or a revision of our established structure of freight terminals.''

"Ben," Jessie said with as much patience as she could muster, "I submit that you are being fractious in this matter. You won't even consider changes or compromise. That is no way to resolve the serious matters facing us and the company.''

"I take the liberty of submitting to you, my dear," Harrison countered in a voice that oozed venom, "that the difficulties facing us could be resolved in one fell swoop, so to speak, if we could but eliminate Mr. Michael Brandon from the scene. It is he who plagues us with his talk of rate reductions and no more evictions

136

and so on. Without him on the scene, things would once again be peaceful, and we could pursue our course with a comfortable expectation of ever-increasing profits, which would make any reasonable person happy, our shareholders very much included.''

"Excuse me, sir," Ki said, his voice deferential, "but I think you might be mistaken about that."

"You think so, do you?" Harrison said, lighting a cigar and blowing smoke toward Ki. "How do you reach that interesting conclusion, pray tell?"

"Mike Brandon isn't the only person who has a low opinion of your railroad."

"You mean, of course, other settlers of his ilk, I suppose," Harrison suggested.

"I had in mind the National Grange of the Patrons of Husbandry."

"Ah, yes, Oliver Hudson Kelley's bunch of farmers," Harrison remarked dismissively through a cloud of cigar smoke, referring to the founder of the organization.

"I wouldn't be so fast to dismiss the Grangers as just 'a bunch of farmers,' " said Ki. "Not when you consider that they have, I recently read somewhere, over one and a half million members scattered around the country in twenty thousand or so lodges. That's a lot of farmers and a lot of power if you look at them as a voting block. They've been running for offices and winning elections. They've also, I've heard, been pretty successful at getting laws passed that limit freight and passenger rates in certain parts of the country."

"More troublemakers," Harrison grumbled. "Like Brandon's gang."

"They could make a lot of trouble for the Southern Pacific in the days to come if people like you and Jessie and the other members of the railroad's board don't lend an ear to them. If they keep up the way they're going, you might find your railroad declared a public utility with its rates set by Congress."

"Ki's right," Jessie told Harrison. "And Mike Brandon has the support of Isaac Pendleton, who is an officer in the local Grange lodge in Fresno County. I witnessed

137

an organized attempt to interfere with one of our trains by the men associated with Pendleton."

"They derailed one of our trains?" Harrison spluttered.

"They were planning to, but Mike—Brandon—persuaded them to block the tracks instead of running the risk of causing injury or worse to people on the train. They are an organization I believe we ignore at our peril, Ben."

"Members of the Grange," Ki pointed out, "are some of your best customers since they ship their harvests to market on your line and are, therefore and naturally, particularly incensed about the present terminal rate. They could very easily turn from your best customers into your worst enemies."

"Speaking of enemies, Ben," Jessie said, "I should tell you that while I was in Fresno County I heard that your chief of security became involved in a shooting during an eviction you apparently sent him to supervise. Chet Langley shot and wounded a man named Amos Copeland, who was the head of the family being evicted."

"Langley told me about that incident. He said he had been threatened and had acted in self-defense."

"That's not the way I heard the story," Jessie said, "but I'll let that go for the moment. Someone also shot at either Brandon or at me, neither of us are sure which. It might have been one of Isaac Pendleton's Grangers who was discontented because Mike—Brandon—had not made good on his threat to kill me in order to force the line to accede to their mutual demands. Or it might have been someone who wanted Brandon out of the way so that Pendleton could take over the leadership of the settlers' struggle.

"I bring the incident up now to show you that serious trouble is brewing, and unless we take direct and prompt action to avert it, the line is going to suffer one way or another—from attacks on our trains to bad publicity that could cause others to rise up in revolt against our policies."

138

"If Brandon had been killed—assuming it was he who was being fired upon," Harrison said stonily, "all our troubles would now be over."

"That is a decidedly simplistic view of things, Ben," Jessie snapped, losing her temper.

"Simple views are usually the clearest ones. Also the most effective ones."

"I take it you are not about to change any of your views?"

"That is correct."

"Then I have no alternative," Jessie said, "but to take unilateral action to alter the company's policies, which I now feel, since I have had firsthand experience with the results of those backward policies, are destructive not only to the people they affect who use our line but also to us as individuals."

"You cannot act unilaterally!" Harrison said, almost shouting. "Only a majority vote of the members of the board can change current policies."

"I shall try to obtain that majority by the simple expedient of calling a special board meeting to explain to the members what they may not know and what I have learned since I was kidnapped—namely, the settlers' side of this sad story, which I happen to think is a legitimate one."

"I'll fight you, Jessie!" an angry Harrison threatened. "You'll not succeed in whatever harm you are planning to do to my railroad."

"*Your* railroad?" an incensed Jessie repeated in disbelief. "The Southern Pacific is not *your* railroad. It belongs to the stockholders and, in a very real sense, to the people of this country that it was built to serve."

"I warn you once again, Jessie," Harrison said, his dead cigar still in his hand but forgotten now. "Whatever you try, I'll fight you every inch of the way, and I'll stop you. In this uncertain world of ours, that is one thing you can count on. *I'll stop you!*"

Ki rose and, after a nod to Harrison, followed Jessie out of the office.

"That man has become insufferable!" Jessie declared

as they emerged onto the crowded street. "Did you hear him? He talks about the Southern Pacific as if it were his own private province to run as he sees fit."

"I encountered the same attitude when I went to see him after you disappeared. I've found that many men become obsessed with the business they engage in. Their companies become the be-all and end-all of their lives. Such, I think, is the case with Mr. Harrison vis-à-vis the railroad."

"A sad state of affairs for any man, in my opinion."

"A potentially dangerous one as well."

"Dangerous?"

"Yes, dangerous," Ki reiterated as they made their way down the street. "Because a man like Harrison, a man obsessed with an enterprise such as the Southern Pacific, and determined to have his way with it come hell or high water, well, there is no telling what such a man might do to achieve his ends. A man like that borders on being a fanatic, and fanatics will usually stop at nothing to further their cause or achieve their goal."

"Well, Ben Harrison reckoned without me."

"Where are we going?"

"I'm going to the telegraph office. I intend to exercise my right as a board member to call a special meeting to discuss the changes I want to see made in the way the line is operated in the future. I'm going to contact each of the board members and convene a meeting as soon as possible. Ki, you needn't come with me. I imagine you want to get back to the Parker House to freshen up, maybe take a nap. We could meet for supper tonight."

"I do want to take a bath, and a nap wouldn't be at all out of order," Ki admitted. "But I think I'll go with you to the telegraph office."

Jessie gave him a sidelong glance. She knew there was more to what he had said than his words had conveyed. She pondered the matter for a moment and then said, "You're coming with me instead of returning to the hotel for a bath and some rest. There must be some reason why you want to do that instead of indulging yourself at the Parker House. I don't think it's just the pleasure of my company that has led you to your choice."

Ki said nothing.

"I think it's because you're afraid something might happen to me if you were to leave me alone. That's it, isn't it?"

"Let's just say that I think it would be a good idea for me to stay by your side as much as possible for the remainder of our stay in San Francisco."

"Stop beating around the bush and give me a straight answer."

Ki smiled at Jessie's impatience. Had they been standing still, he was sure she would have stamped her foot to express her annoyance. "You're right. I think it's possible that something might happen to you if I were to leave you alone."

"What might happen? You think Mike Brandon will try to kidnap me again?"

"You smile at the idea, but I don't think it's a possibility to be dismissed or taken so lightly. Brandon did it once. He very well might try it again."

"It didn't work for him the first time. Harrison did nothing to meet his demands."

"If at first you don't succeed . . ." Ki let his words trail away.

"If Brandon tries to kidnap me again, I'll—" I'll what? Jessie asked herself. Fight him off? Throw myself into his arms and go gladly with him? The mixed emotions she was experiencing at the thought of seeing Mike Brandon again, mixed as they were with her memories of his hard body pressing against her own, momentarily confused her.

"Brandon's not the only one we have to worry about now," Ki said pointedly.

"You mean I have to worry about what Ben Harrison might do?"

"He said he'd stop you from making the changes you want to make in the way the railroad's run."

"Surely you don't think he'd do anything drastic?"

141

"I told you before that I think the man is something of a fanatic. Fanatics are unpredictable."

"You make me feel guilty. I'm keeping you from such purely sensual pleasures as a hot bath and a nice nap."

"They can wait."

Minutes later Jessie pointed and said, "There it is."

They entered the telegraph office together, and Jessie sat down to compose the message she intended to send to each of the men who served as directors of the Southern Pacific Company.

After sending the messages, she and Ki left the telegraph office and started to make their way to the Parker House. Halfway there Jessie suddenly stopped.

"What's wrong?" Ki asked her, looking around to see what might have brought his friend to a halt.

"I was just thinking that holding a special meeting of the board of directors may or may not accomplish what I want to do. A majority of them might not agree with me. Ben might prevail upon most of them to side with him and vote down my proposals."

"What else can you do to be sure you win in the end?"

Jessie smiled. "There are distinct advantages in being a very rich woman when push comes to shove, Ki. Follow me."

Ki followed Jessie to the San Francisco stock exchange, where she was, upon identifying herself, ushered into a plush sitting room full of mahogany furniture and lush carpets and red velvet drapes.

They had no sooner taken seats in the opulent room than a young man entered through another door and declared, "A pleasure to see you again, Miss Starbuck. What can we do for you this time? We are, of course, at your service as always."

"Good day, Mr. Smythe," Jessie said. "It's been some time since I did business with you directly like this, but let me say that it is a genuine pleasure to have the opportunity to do so."

"You are most kind, Miss Starbuck."

"I would like to buy some stock."

Smythe went to a table, opened a drawer, took out

some printed forms, a quill pen, and an inkwell, and carried them across the room to another larger table, where he sat down. Arranging the papers on the table before him, he looked up expectantly. "What would you like to buy, Miss Starbuck?"

"Shares of the stock of the Southern Pacific Company."

Smythe was about to begin filling out one of the forms when he stopped and looked up at Jessie. "As I recall, you own quite a few shares in the company already. There may be other issues that you might find more—"

"I have always appreciated your advice, Mr. Smythe, but this time I really can't use it, because, you see, I've already made up my mind. I want to buy as many shares of Southern Pacific as I possibly can the moment they come on the market."

"Of course, Miss Starbuck. What price range do you have in mind?"

"The price is of no importance this time, Mr. Smythe. Buy the shares at whatever price you have to pay to obtain them. I want to become the majority stockholder in the company, and I want that to happen as soon as possible."

"As I recall, you presently own thirty—or is it thirty-five—percent of the company's outstanding shares?"

"Nearly forty percent, Mr. Smythe."

"Will there be anything else at this time, Miss Starbuck?" Smythe inquired, busily filling out forms.

"That will be all, thank you." Jessie rose. "It was very nice doing business with you again, Mr. Smythe. I wonder, would you send word to me periodically at the Parker House as you make the buys for me? I'm eager to know when I own fifty-one percent of the company."

"I shall be happy to keep you posted on the progress we are making in achieving your investment goals, Miss Starbuck."

Once outside the exchange, Ki said, "Well, it would seem that there is more than one way to skin a skunk."

143

Jessie, feigning shock, declared, "What would Ben Harrison say if he had heard you refer to him in such an unkind, not to mention uncouth, manner?"

They were laughing as they headed for the Parker House.

Later, as they were crossing the hotel's lobby, Ki noticed the woman who was standing some distance away with her back to him.

She was talking to a middle-aged man and switching her weight from leg to leg as she did so. There was something vaguely familiar about her, he thought. Then, as she patted her ringleted raven hair with one coquettish hand, he remembered her. The working woman he had picked up—or had she picked him up?—the night he had first arrived at the Parker House with Jessie. Her name was—he thought for a moment—Opal.

"You go ahead," he told Jessie. "There's something I want to take care of. I'll join you for supper later as we planned, all right?"

"Fine. See you later."

Ki crossed the lobby to where the middle-aged man was backing away from Opal, his face flushed, and saying something about not being able to, not right now, his wife . . .

Opal, as her flustered potential customer turned and hurried away from her, also turned—and found herself face to face with Ki.

"Oh," she said, giving him a welcoming smile. "It's you."

"It is."

"So you're still here at the hotel."

"I am."

"I haven't seen you during the last few days."

"I was out of town. On business. Shall we go up to my room?"

She took his arm and walked with him to the elevator.

Once inside his room with the door closed, she cocked her head to one side and asked, "What's it to be this time? The same as before? Or something different?"

144

"A little bit of both," he replied. "Something old, something new."

She smiled and dropped down on her knees before him. Her fingers deftly unbuttoned his trousers, and her lips as deftly took his stone-stiff shaft into her hot mouth.

Ki groaned with pleasure as her tongue began to lave the underside of his manhood. He did what he would have considered impossible only a moment ago. He became even stiffer. His erection slid in and out of her mouth as she sucked skillfully on it, and he gloried in her lips' caress and her tongue's teasing.

He let it go on for a minute longer, but then, taking her head in his hands, he withdrew from her mouth, fearful that if he didn't—if he let it go on any longer—he would climax, and he didn't want to do that, not this time. This time he wanted . . .

He began to undress and so did Opal. When they were both naked, they lay down side by side on the bed. Then Ki rolled over upon her and positioned himself so that his shaft stabbed between her thighs. He cupped her face in his hands and then lowered his hands to fondle her plump breasts. His thumbs toyed with her nipples. He eased his body down along hers and then began to suck her right breast, his tongue and teeth causing her to moan softly and turn her head from side to side. He switched to her left breast and repeated what he had just done while his right hand roamed down over her silken skin and came to rest against the thatched mound between her legs.

He stroked her there while still sucking her right breast, and then he eased his middle finger into her. He found her warm and moist and, moments later, hot and wet. He raised his head and looked down at her. Her eyes were closed. Her lips were parted. Her chest heaved as she breathed.

He withdrew his fingers and mounted her. Supporting himself on his hands, he looked down and then thrust his shaft into her. As he probed her, her arms encircled him, and her hands come to rest on his back. He dropped down upon her and plunged all the way into her, holding himself rigid upon her, feeling her embrace envelop him.

Then, slowly and in what he intended to be a tantalizing manner, he raised his hips, lowered them, raised them again. He used his legs to force hers farther apart as he continued his deliberately slow rhythm that was causing her, as he slid almost all the way out of her, to thrust her own loins upward in an eager, almost savage manner as she sought—fought—to maintain his swollen flesh within her.

A tingling sensation slid up and down his spine. Every nerve in his body seemed to him to be awake now and singing an aroused song that was bringing his blood to a hot boil and causing all ten of his toes to curl.

He slid his arms under her body and clasped her to him, his lips nuzzling her neck, as ecstasy was born in his body and he felt himself beginning to spin out of this world and into a wildly erotic wonderland.

Beneath him, Opal was bucking as furiously as he was, crying out a moment later as she experienced an orgasm. As her loins continued to slap sweatily against Ki's, he exploded and flowed hotly into her, uttering a moan as an intense wave of pleasure washed throughout his entire body.

He was still bucking uncontrollably and flooding her a moment later when she climaxed a second time and gave a little cry that shrilled past his ear. Her fingernails clawed at his back.

Then, slowly, he began to drift down from the ecstatic heights he had reached. His body gave a single final shudder and then became still. His heart still raced, but it no longer pounded within his chest like a prisoner determined to escape. He groaned, then sighed contentedly. The sweat on his body began to cool. The fire that had been burning in his shaft slowly subsided into embers.

When he withdrew from her, she gave a little grunt of vague protest as she lay with her eyes shut and both of her arms thrown outward.

Ki flopped down beside her on the bed. He lay there

on his back staring up at the ceiling and luxuriating in the spent feeling that had swept over him, leaving him totally satisfied and completely relaxed.

"It's men like you who make my profession rewarding," Opal whispered to him and playfully tweaked his ear.

"That's a compliment if I ever heard one."

"Are you up to another go—free of charge this time?"

"Look at it," Ki said, laughing. "It's not only up; it never did go down."

"Want to try it this way?" Opal asked as she rolled over on her stomach and thrust her buttocks up into the air.

Why not? Ki thought and sent his shaft plunging into the tunnel it had so recently left. This time, because of the positions he and Opal had assumed, he went in even deeper. Opal's moans were deeper this time, too, as he thrust rapidly and vigorously, burying himself within her and bringing her almost immediately to a climax. She achieved still another orgasm before Ki surged into her, spilling a torrent of hot lava from the fiery volcano his body had become.

This time, when they separated, Opal, breathless, lay limply beside him. Her lips parted and she whispered, "That was even better than the first time."

Jessie sat, with her hair pinned on top of her head, in a tin bathtub in her hotel room luxuriating in the hot soapy water that filled it. The heat of the water so soothed her body that she relaxed, closed her eyes, and almost dozed.

Then, sitting up straight in the tub, she proceeded to lather her body with soap and then rinse it all away. When she stepped out of the tub some time later, she proceeded to towel herself dry. The vigorous rubbing she gave herself brought a rosy glow to her smooth skin.

When she was thoroughly dry, she put on her dressing gown and unpinned her hair, letting it fall in a coppery shower around her shoulders. She was brushing it with a series of steady strokes, when a knock sounded on the door. Ki, she thought. But wasn't it really too early for him to arrive for their supper date? The bellboy, then, come to empty the tub and carry it away just as he had brought and filled it for her earlier. She went to the door and was about to open it when she recalled Ki's remark about not wanting to leave her alone and the reasons he had given her for feeling the way he did. There was probably no need for her to be cautious, but, she decided, there certainly was no harm in being so.

"Who is it?" she called out.

"A message for Miss Starbuck," a male voice answered from beyond the door.

Jessie unlocked and opened the door.

She stared at the two men standing in the hall, one of whom she knew. "What do you want?" she asked them.

"You," was the familiar man's answer, which made Jessie experience a disquieting sense that this had all happened to her before. A moment later, when the man she knew said, "You're coming with us. Get dressed. Move!", she knew she had lived through this scene before, when she had been kidnapped from this same room.

She tried to slam the door in the faces of the two men in the hall, but the one she knew put out a hand and stopped her from doing so. Both men then entered her room, shoving her before them, as the other man said, "Don't scream, lady. If you do, you're dead."

As he closed the door, Jessie went to the bed, where she had earlier laid out clean clothes, and taking off her dressing gown, she began to dress. She kept her back to the two men who had invaded her room and tried to ignore her feeling of embarrassment which bordered on humiliation as she was forced to stand naked, however briefly, in front of the pair. But she had known there would be no point in asking them to turn their backs on her. They wouldn't because they would be afraid she might attempt to escape from them.

Escape.

She glanced at the open window. The lace curtain covering it moved in the light breeze coming through the window. Her gaze shifted to the top of her bureau, on which rested a spool of thread, a needle, and a pair of

148

sewing scissors, all of which she had used before taking her bath to mend several tears in the clothes she had been wearing during her earlier captivity in Fresno County.

She continued dressing, but apparently not fast enough to suit the men behind her.

"Hurry it up, lady," one of them barked, and the other said, "We like watching the show you're giving us, but we've got more important things to do, so get a move on."

Jessie buttoned a final button on her blouse, adjusted her skirt, and went over to the bureau.

"Let's go," the man she knew said sharply.

"I have to get a handkerchief." She opened the top drawer of the bureau. But she did not reach into it for a handkerchief. Instead, she took the scissors from the top of the bureau, spun around, and stabbed the man she knew, who was standing closest to her. As her scissors bit into his left hand, he set out a cry of pain and reached out to seize her. But Jessie was already running toward the open window, intending to climb through it and out onto the roof, where she planned to jump down to the ground.

But the other man in the room was too quick for her. Before she reached the window, he tackled her, and they both went down, hitting the floor hard. Stunned by her fall, she nevertheless tried to stab him with her scissors, but he was too strong and quickly overpowered her. As he dragged her, still struggling, to her feet, the man she had stabbed strode up to her and, cursing furiously, gave her a right uppercut with his uninjured hand, which snapped her head backward and knocked her unconscious.

★

Chapter 9

After Opal had been paid and had left his hotel room, Ki arranged, as Jessie had done earlier, for a bath. When it was ready, he stripped and climbed into the tin tub and sat there soaking for several minutes, his mind roaming through thrilling memories of Opal. He imagined he could feel the touch of her lips, her hands. He could see again in his mind's eye her voluptuous breasts and enticing body. He hoped he would be able to get together with her again. He would make it a point to do so, he decided, if he possibly could.

But for now she would live in his memory. He proceeded to busy himself with the task at hand—freeing his body of the dirt and grime of his train rides and also of the sweat that his energetic encounter with Opal had wrung from his pores.

By the time he had finished bathing and had dried himself, he was ravenously hungry. As he dressed in clean clothes, his mouth watered and his stomach rumbled. Once dressed, he took a final look at himself in the mirror and then left his room, locking the door behind him.

He knocked on Jessie's door and stood there in the hall whistling a tune as he tried to take his mind off his hunger. He knocked again when no one answered the door. He began to feel a distinct sense of uneasiness when he received no response to his second louder knock. It couldn't be, he told himself. But he knew it very well could be. Jessie could be in trouble again. He should have stood guard outside her door, he told himself when he tried the knob and the unlocked door swung open. He entered the room with trepidation and found exactly what he feared he would find—nothing. No Jessie.

But his keen eyes did spot the drops of dried blood on the beige carpeting. A moment later he discovered the bloody sewing scissors behind a chair.

Blood on the floor. Bloody scissors.

They told him a cryptic story, one which had any number of possible plots. Had she accidentally hurt herself with the scissors? Had someone used them to hurt her? Or was she now downstairs in the dining room or gaming room waiting for him?

He hurriedly left the room and made his way downstairs, aware of the fact that he had done the same thing once before. Now he was doing it again, and he worried that this time he might find as equally disturbing an explanation for what he had seen in her room as the one he had received the first time in somewhat similiar circumstances.

"Yes, sir?" the cheerful desk clerk greeted him as he approached the desk.

"I'm looking for Miss Jessica Starbuck. Have you seen her?"

"No, sir, I haven't."

"Has she left any message for me? My name is Ki." He gave the man his room number.

The clerk turned to a wall rack behind him and checked the pigeonhole in it that bore the same number as Ki's room.

"No, sir, there are no messages here for you."

Ki turned and hurried into the dining room, scanning the faces of the people who had gathered for an early supper. Jessie was not among them. He made his way into the gaming room and walked quickly through the crowds of people filling it. When he still had not located Jessie, he halted, thinking of what to do next.

He went back to the desk and asked the clerk how long he had been on duty. "Since three o'clock this afternoon, sir," was the man's answer.

"Have you been here all the time? Could Miss Starbuck have come into and then left the lobby without your having seen her?"

"Oh, no, sir. I think that's highly unlikely. As you can see, we have a full view of the lobby and the front door from the desk."

"There must be a back door to the hotel."

"There is one, sir. It's that way—turn left at the elevators, and you'll find the kitchen at the end of a short corridor."

Ki left the desk and went down the corridor, which was out of the desk clerk's line of sight. He pushed open the swinging doors and entered the kitchen. He saw the hotel's back door directly ahead of him on the far side of the room. It was partially hidden by billowing clouds of steam rising from the many pots boiling on the huge stove. He went to it, opened it, and found himself peering into an empty alleyway that ran behind the hotel. He turned and seized the arm of a white-hatted chef.

"Did you see one of the guests—a strikingly attractive woman—come through here within the past several hours?"

"The woman I saw wasn't very attractive when she came through here," the chef said and shook his arm free. "The two men with her had all they could do to get her out into the alley back there. She was close to dead drunk. They practically had to drag her out of here. I guess they didn't want her to be seen in the lobby in her inebriated condition."

"Did she have copper-colored hair? Green eyes?"

"Her hair—yeah, I suppose you could call it copper-

153

colored. As for her eyes—I didn't see them. They were closed.''

"How long ago did you see her and the two men with her?"

The chef pondered for a moment. "Let's see. I was chopping clams for the chowder—"

"*How long ago did you see her!*" Ki shouted.

"About an hour ago, I'd say. Yeah, about an hour ago, give or take five or ten minutes."

"Did you see which way they went when they left here?"

The chef shook his head. "It was so busy in here when they came through that I could barely see the nose in front of my face, never mind which way they went."

Ki turned and went out into the alley, thinking: She wasn't drunk. I've never seen Jessie drunk as long as I've known her.

He began walking down the alley, lost in thought and consumed by worry.

"Sir! I say, sir!"

He turned around to find the desk clerk beckoning to him. He retraced his steps.

"Sir," said the desk clerk, "there is a gentleman here to see you. He asked for your room number only a little while after you inquired about Miss Starbuck. I told him that you weren't in your room but that I could locate you. I came to the kitchen, and the chef told me you had gone out into the alley."

"Who is the gentleman?"

"He didn't give me his name, sir. If you'll just follow me—"

Ki followed the clerk back to the lobby desk, where he was surprised to find Benjamin Harrison waiting for him.

"Ki," Harrison said in a strained voice and offered his hand.

Ki shook it as Harrison said, "He's done it again."

"Who's done what again?"

"Brandon. He's kidnapped Jessie again—or had her kidnapped. I was just about to close our offices for the

154

day when a messenger arrived with a note.'' Harrison rummaged about in his pocket and came up with a folded piece of paper, which he handed to Ki.

Ki took it from him, unfolded it, and began to read the scrawled message that was written in pencil.

I've got her and I mean to keep her until such time as you meet our demands. You've got two days from the time you receive this message. If you haven't met our demands by that time, Jessie Starbuck dies.

"What are you going to do?'' Ki asked as he stared at the note that had been signed: Mike Brandon.

"I don't know what I can do. I'm certainly not going to be bullied into altering sound and proven business practices in the face of Brandon's threats. I came to you as soon as I received the note. I thought, since you were successful in finding Brandon and rescuing Jessie before, you might succeed this time as well.''

"Last time I didn't have a deadline to meet,'' Ki pointed out. "Brandon says he'll kill her in two days if you don't give in to him. I think you have no choice but to do just that, Harrison. If you don't—well, you read the note.''

"As I told you the last time we went over this same ground, Ki, my hands are tied. I cannot and I will not risk the ruin of the Southern Pacific Railroad to appease criminals like the two men, whoever they were, who kidnapped Jessie.''

Ki angrily reached out and seized the lapels of Harrison's coat. Pulling the man close to him—so close, in fact, that their noses were nearly touching—he said, "You've *got* to meet Brandon's demands, Harrison. I know you and Jessie are at loggerheads at the moment about what to do about the settlers and the terminal rate and so on, but forget about all that. Remember that Jessie's life is at stake here. You've got to give in to Brandon this time for Jessie's sake, and you've got to do it before

155

his deadline passes and he decides to make good on his threat.''

Harrison angrily shook himself free of Ki. ''I'll do no such thing. I'm sorry that Jessie has been kidnapped again. You should have protected her, since you are her close friend. *She* should have been more careful. She should have learned from her previous experience and avoided danger at all costs. I'm sorry that Jessie is once again in jeopardy. But I must point out that she is but one person, and her plight must not be allowed to bring the Southern Pacific to its knees. The railroad must survive at all costs. It is far more important than any one individual, myself included. No, I will not surrender. To do so would be to free Jessie but place the line itself as a hostage in the hands of the likes of Mike Brandon.''

''*Damn* you, Harrison!'' Ki muttered through clenched teeth. ''I'm leaving now. I'm going to find Brandon, and I'm going to kill him and anybody else who tries to harm Jessie. But I'll tell you something. What I would really like to do is start my killing spree right now with you as my first victim.''

''Why, I never!'' Harrison exclaimed, his eyes widening in alarm. ''If I had known I was going to receive such a violent reception, I never would have bothered to come here to tell you that Jessie had been kidnapped.''

''Get out of here, Harrison, before I—''

Harrison turned and ran from Ki, his coattails flapping behind him as he fled out into the street, one hand holding his hat on his head.

Consciousness returned to Jessie slowly and in the fragmented form of a series of stark images and still starker memories.

The first flying toward her face and the pain it brought with it that had knocked her senseless . . . sight and sound gradually returning to her . . . a man's voice saying ''put her under'' . . . a cloth being pressed against her nose—the sickly sweet smell of chloroform fumes in her nostrils as she gasped for fresh air . . . now this . . .

This was a dingy room somewhere, she didn't know

156

where. No pictures hung on the bare wooden walls. The room was filled with shadows instead of furniture. She was lying on the floor, her hands bound behind her back. Her jaw was sore as a result of the blow that had landed on it in her hotel room. How long ago had that been? She had no way of knowing. It could have been minutes or days ago.

She managed to get herself into a sitting position. Then she stood up. Her head throbbed as a result of the chloroform that had been forced upon her.

She walked stiffly toward the room's only window and leaned heavily against the boards covering it. She couldn't budge them. She turned around and headed for the door that faced her on the far side of the room. Turning her back to it, she tried to turn its knob with her bound hands. It wouldn't turn. Locked, she thought. She kicked the door several times in quick succession.

Moments later she heard the sound of a key in the lock. She stepped back as the door swung open and Chet Langley, Ben Harrison's chief of security, stepped into the room.

"What's all the racket about?" Langley asked.

"Where am I?"

"Never you mind about where you are. It doesn't much matter since you won't be here all that long."

"I take it Ben Harrison put you up to kidnapping me."

"He did, yes. I got the distinct impression from Mr. Harrison that you and he haven't been exactly seeing eye-to-eye lately on things he considers important."

"Why did he have you bring me here?"

"To stop you from making trouble for him, that's why. Why else? Did you think he wanted to keep you locked up here like his own little lady in a private little love nest?" When Jessie didn't answer, Langley continued, "That might not be such a bad idea, come to think of it." He gave Jessie a smile that was more of a leer.

"I thought the railroad paid you to serve as Mr. Harrison's chief of security, not as his private kidnapper."

"I'm a man of many talents, which is why Mr. Harrison and I get along together as famously as we do."

"When I get out of here," Jessie said, "both you and Ben Harrison are going to rue the day you ever did this to me. I'll see that you both land in jail for most of the rest of your lives."

"When you get out of here? You're not getting out of here. Not alive, you're not."

Langley's words sent a chill coursing through Jessie, but she tried to maintain an impassive expression so that Langley would not see the fear she was feeling.

"Where is Ben Harrison?" she asked.

"Oh, around, I should say. I can't tell you where for sure, but he ought to be showing up here pretty soon."

"I want to talk to him the minute he arrives."

"I'll be sure to tell him that. Meanwhile, why don't you just sit down and keep quiet. My partner, Jim Bisbee, he doesn't like noise. So, like I said, keep it toned down, hear? By the way, bitch, you did me up fair and fine with that little scissors of yours, you did. It still hurts like hell where you stabbed me."

Langley held up his hand which was wrapped in a bloody bandage made out of a dirty piece of muslin. "I'm looking forward to evening out the score between you and me, and that evening out, it'll not be long in coming, I can tell you."

Langley left the room, slammed the door, and locked it, leaving Jessie alone with her thoughts.

They were not pleasant ones. She had no doubt now that Harrison intended to have her killed. Of course, it was entirely possible that Langley had been bluffing on that point, but she strongly doubted it. He might have just been trying to put a scare into her. But somehow she knew, deep within herself, that he did fully intend to kill her. How? she wondered. When?

Such thoughts were intolerable. She tried to push them aside, tried to concentrate on something else. But that didn't seem to be possible. The fearful thoughts kept returning however hard she tried to fight them off.

She went back to the window and once again tried to pry loose one of the boards covering it. She was unable to do so. Still, she kept trying, working with her bound

158

hands, unable to see what she was doing as she was doing it. She concentrated on the fact that she had to get out of here—wherever *here* was. And she had to do it soon before Harrison could unleash his pair of dogs— Chet Langley and Jim Bisbee—and they did whatever he would order them to do to her.

She cried out in pain as slivers sliced into two of her fingers from the board she was trying to loosen. But she kept at it, despite the pain in her fingers and the blood seeping from them, which gradually made the wood she was attacking slippery.

She was still at it when she heard voices coming from beyond the door of the room in which she was imprisoned. Voices coming closer to that door. Then the key was turning in the lock, the harsh sound of metal against metal that seemed to resound in the quiet air of the room.

"Ah, there you are, my dear," Ben Harrison said as he stepped into the room, doffed his hat, and gave Jessie a courtly bow. "I understand you have been a naughty, naughty girl. I understand that you stabbed Chet Langley with scissors and that you tried to do the same to Jim Bisbee when he was chloroforming you.

"By the way, that little charade that Langley and Bisbee put on—they told me all about it—must have really been something to see. I'm so sorry to have missed it. They told me they pretended you were drunk and that they pretended to be good Samaritans helping you out of the hotel by way of its kitchen to spare you embarrassment. A most amusing little farce, that, and one that proved to be quite successful."

"Ben, I never thought I'd live to see the day that you'd stoop to kidnapping to attain your goals," Jessie declared.

"Didn't you, my dear? Well, now you have seen just such a day dawn. I really think you shouldn't be surprised. Don't you recall the things I told you the night you and your friend Ki and I dined at the Occidental Restaurant following your arrival in San Francisco?"

Without waiting for an answer from Jessie, Harrison continued, "Let me refresh your memory, if I may. I

159

told you then that I was and always have been deeply involved in the fortunes of the Southern Pacific almost from the first day on my first job with the line as a tracklayer. I recall saying to you that evening that the railroad's interests became my interests. Do you remember that conversation, Jessie?''

''I do.''

''Then you'll recall that I said at the time that the railroad's friends became my friends.'' Harrison paused. Then, he added, ''I also said that its enemies became my enemies.''

''You view me as your enemy because of the disagreements existing between us, I take it.''

''But you *are* my enemy, Jessie. Surely I've explained my view of things clearly enough so that you can understand that I cannot tolerate interference in the line's fortunes whether that interference comes from a lowly settler like Michael Brandon or a member of my own board of directors like yourself.''

Jessie recalled the intensity and almost wild-eyed enthusiasm with which Harrison had spoken the night of their dinner together to which he had just referred. She remembered him saying then that he considered the Southern Pacific—how had he put it? ''*A loving if sometimes harsh mistress who demands her due, which I am and have always been willing to give her.*'' As she recalled that statement and others like it that Harrison had so firmly made at the time, she thought she saw a way to appeal to him that might get her out of the dangerous predicament in which she found herself.

''Ben, I understand how you feel, and I share your feelings, I really do,'' she began.

He frowned. ''You don't. If you did, you would not have come to me proposing such nonsense as a reduction in the terminal rate and a halt to the eviction of settlers who refuse to pay a fair price for the land the railroad has let them use at no charge all these years.''

''I don't want to harm the line in any way, Ben. I just want to reach a fair compromise with the people the line's policies are adversely affecting.''

160

"I want to hear no more about it. No more. Not one *word*!"

Jessie saw the fire flare in Harrison's eyes as he made his angry statement. She saw the manic expression that had taken over his face and twisted his features into a mask of boiling rage.

"Soon you will pose no further threat to the Southern Pacific," he told her. "Soon you will be but an obnoxious memory, and things can go on the way they were before you arrived in San Francisco and promptly proceeded to cause trouble for everyone."

She was afraid to ask the question that was now in the forefront of her mind. Or, rather, afraid of what Harrison's answer to it might be. She nevertheless put it into words: "What are you going to do with me?"

Harrison smiled a smile Jessie thought would do credit to a snake.

"I am going to have you killed."

His answer hung in the air between them like a sword poised to plunge into Jessie's heart.

"There will be a delicious irony in your death, my dear. Shall I tell you about it?"

Jessie didn't want to hear any more. On the other hand, she wanted to stall for time, in the hope that something would happen that might give her a fighting chance to escape from Harrison.

"Tell me," she said in a dull voice.

"I've just come from visiting your friend, Ki."

The mention of Ki's name gave Jessie hope. Maybe he would find her and rescue her as he had done when Brandon had kidnapped her.

"I gave Ki a note, to which I added Michael Brandon's signature, which stated that he had kidnapped you a second time and intended to kill you if the railroad did not change its policies. That note made Ki very angry, as I had expected it would. He was so angry at the thought that Brandon had brazenly dared to kidnap you a second time that he vowed—I heard him do so with my very own ears—to find and kill Brandon and anyone else who might attempt to harm you.

161

"Isn't that a perfectly lovely irony? Ki, in a noble effort to rescue you once again from the man he believes to be the villain of this piece, is going to kill Brandon, the principal enemy of the Southern Pacific."

Jessie's heart sank.

"I feel quite confident that Ki will manage to kill Brandon. But, should he fail to do so for any reason, Brandon will wind up in prison. I've little doubt about that."

"Mike in prison? Why?"

"Because, my dear, when they find your corpse, and they learn from Ki that he rescued you once from Brandon only to have you kidnapped again by the same arch villain—all the evidence will point to Brandon as your murderer. The police will be convinced of his guilt, and I, who arranged your death to suit my own purposes, will remain free as a bird to blithely continue running the Southern Pacific as I see fit."

"Ben, this is insane."

"It's *not* insane!" Harrison roared. "*I* am not insane. I have given much thought to this matter since you last visited my office. I have been able to find no other suitable course of action but to dispose of you and Brandon both. Only then will the threat to the line I love be removed. It is, one might say, akin to a surgical procedure. I am simply excising two malignant growths, you and Brandon, either of which could, if left unattended to, destroy the company I love."

Jessie realized that there was no hope of reasoning with Harrison. But she nevertheless felt she had to make one last try. "Ben, what you're doing is making trouble, not eliminating it. Your actions have already led to my kidnapping by Mike Brandon and to people in Fresno County shooting at each other."

"Your latter remark refers, I assume, to the unknown assailant who, you told me, shot at either you or Brandon."

"Yes, I refer to that incident as well as to the shooting of a settler named Amos Copeland by Chet Langley, which I told you about the last time we talked."

162

Harrison laughed shrilly. "That unknown someone was shooting at you, Jessie. His name was Chet Langley. I sent him there to find you and kill you."

Jessie blanched at Harrison's announcement.

"Unfortunately, he failed in his mission. But I will not fail in mine. *Langley!*"

Jessie, a feeling of desperation welling up within her, knew she had to act. But, with her hands bound, there was little she could do. However, there was one thing that she hoped might work.

She took a step toward Harrison, and before he could back away from her, she raised her right leg, bent it at the knee, and then sent it flying forward toward Harrison. Her foot caught him high up on the chest and doubled him over. As he gasped for breath, she brought her knee up, and it struck his chin with a resounding crack of bone against bone.

As Harrison crumpled to the floor and lay there in a helpless heap, Jessie dashed through the door—and into the strong arms of Chet Langley.

"I got her Mr. Harrison!" he called out gleefully, a smirk on his face as Jessie twisted and turned, trying to free herself from him.

He half-dragged, half-carried her back into the room, where he stopped and stared down in amazement at Harrison, who lay moaning on the floor in a fetal position.

"Bisbee!" Langley yelled, and when his colleague had joined him, he said, "Hold on to her while I help Mr. Harrison."

Bisbee got a firm grip on Jessie's left arm and watched as Langley helped Harrison stand up.

"Are you okay now, Mr. Harrison?" Langley inquired solicitously. "What'd she do to you?"

"I'm all right. But she won't be for much longer! She kicked me and nearly broke my jaw!"

Harrison strode over to Jessie and backhanded her, snapping her head from one side to the other. "Take her downstairs," he ordered.

Langley went to her and took hold of her right arm. He and Bisbee then marched her out of the room and

163

down a flight of stairs to a rickety landing and then down more stairs until they entered the cellar of the building.

Harrison arrived in the cellar a moment later. "Tie her to that upright over there," he ordered. He watched in silence then as Langley and Bisbee proceeded to carry out his order.

When they had done so, Jessie, her hands still tied behind her, was also bound by strong ropes, which encircled her torso and legs and bound her to the upright supporting the cellar's sagging ceiling.

"Do you notice the dampness in the air, my dear?" Harrison asked her. "That is due to the fact that this building—an abandoned warehouse, incidentally—was once in the very heart of the city's commercial district. But the years passed and the vagaries of the ocean's tides have shifted that district farther inland, leaving this old building to suffer the not-so-tender mercies of the tides."

"I don't know what you're babbling about," Jessie said.

"I am saying that the cellar of this abandoned building that is no longer of interest or value to anyone is periodically flooded at the times of high tide."

Jessie's anger faded as understanding of the fate that awaited her swept down upon her. It was replaced by a cold fear that threatened to overwhelm her. But she forced herself to remain calm. She would not beg Ben Harrison for mercy. She would not abase herself before him.

"I have heard it said that drowning is not a pleasant death," he said softly. "Quite the contrary, in fact. They say that a drowning person's life flashes before him—all of it—in the final few moments before his watery death. You have something to look forward to, my dear. The panorama of a life lived fully, but one that is soon to end.

"You will be able to watch the water slowly rise as the tide comes in. First it will be little more than a thin sheet of water covering the floor. Gradually it will rise above your ankles. Then it will reach your knees. You will probably begin to scream for help by the time it reaches your thighs. You might as well save your breath, which you will soon need. There is no one anywhere nearby to hear you. You will weep when it reaches your chin. You will die when it eventually rises above your head.''

Harrison turned and began to climb the stairs leading out of the cellar. Langley and Bisbee both gave Jessie a final glance before following on the heels of their employer.

Jessie looked down at the floor and saw the faint traces of rotting seaweed scattered about on the rotting wooden floor. She strained against the ropes that held her prisoner. They held firm.

★

Chapter 10

Ki sat tensely in his seat early the next morning as the Southern Pacific train sped southward. His thoughts were focused on one man—Mike Brandon. The man he intended to find. The man who had once again placed the life of his best friend in jeopardy.

"Ticket, sir."

Ki handed the conductor his ticket. "How much longer before we get to Groveland?"

"Not long," the conductor replied, taking a watch from his vest pocket and snapping it open. "Another twenty-two minutes and we should be there."

Twenty-two minutes, Ki thought as the conductor continued collecting tickets. A lifetime. He was keenly aware of the fact that Brandon had set a deadline of two days for the Southern Pacific to bow to his demands or Jessie would die. He feared that Brandon's deadline gave him far too little time to do what he had to do, which was find Brandon and get Jessie away from him.

I'll find him, Ki vowed. I won't let him hurt Jessie. He shifted position in his seat, trying to make himself comfortable. He could not seem to do so no matter which way he turned or twisted.

Suddenly he realized what he was doing. I must live in the here and now, he told himself. But he had been living in the future. At the point in time when he would once again come face to face with Brandon and the man would learn that he had met his match. That was the source of his restlessness, he realized, and that kind of behavior was in total opposition to the way he had been trained.

He recalled the words that his *sensei*, his Japanese master in the study of the martial arts, had often quoted.

Flow with whatever may happen and let your mind be free. Stay centered by accepting whatever you are doing. This is the ultimate.

The words echoed now in his mind. I am sitting here on this train while I travel to my destiny, Ki silently told himself. I must do well at the sitting. He centered his mind on that fact. It wasn't easy. At first, thoughts of Brandon and worries about Jessie intruded on his consciousness. But each time one or the other did, he forced himself to think only of what he was doing at the moment. In time a kind of comforting peace descended upon him, and it was still with him when the conductor announced the train's arrival at the Groveland depot.

It was a calm and self-controlled Ki who stepped down from the train a few minutes later and made his way to the livery barn, where the farrier greeted him as if he had been an old friend.

"I want to rent a horse," Ki told the man. "The one I had last time will be fine if he's available."

The black stallion was, and it was not long before Ki was aboard it and galloping out of town toward the cabin where he had previously confronted Brandon and rescued Jessie.

He rode at a steady pace, the horse beneath him taking long strides and showing no signs of strain. As he approached a bend beyond which was Brandon's cabin, he

168

slowed his mount and then drew rein. Stepping down from the saddle, he led the black over to a red maple sapling and secured it to the tree. Leaving the horse behind him, he made his way through some trees, beneath which was a heavy growth of underbrush. As he rounded the bend, he found himself reciting in his mind the five sins of the ninja warrior mind.

Recklessness, which leads to destruction. Cowardice, which leads to capture. A hot temper that is easily provoked. A sense of honor stimulated by guilt. A worrying temperament.

He intended to commit none of those five sins. He would not be reckless in his attack. He certainly would not be cowardly about it. He was neither hot-tempered nor worried, and he had no sense of honor arising out of a feeling of guilt about what he was about to do.

By the time he had run across an open space between the trees and the blind side of the cabin, he had made up his mind about what he would do. He would make a direct assault, and its impact, if he was successful, would have to be like that of a stone thrown against an egg, terrible at the onset and quick to finish. Brandon would have no chance to prepare. No chance to even react.

Ki moved swiftly around to the front of the cabin and kicked open the door. He was inside in an instant, hands up and ready to attack.

But the cabin was empty.

Ki maintained his warrior's stance for a moment, only his eyes moving. Then he slowly lowered his hands. He went to the hearth and felt the ashes in it. Cold. He went to the cupboard and opened it. No supplies inside. It was apparent to him that Brandon had deserted the cabin.

He fought off a feeling of despair. He could not afford such negative emotions. Not now, when so much was at stake. He had to maintain a positive attitude. He had to act positively as well. But in what way? He didn't like to think of having to return to town and begin asking questions concerning Brandon's whereabouts. He would probably get exactly where he had gotten the last time he had pursued that course—namely, nowhere. But there was one other course of action open to him. He had his doubts about whether it would be a successful or even a wise one. But Helen Simmons's homestead was closer to him now than was the town, and although she had refused to tell him where Brandon was the two times he had been with her, he thought he might be able to persuade her to do so this time—if she knew where his quarry was. If she wouldn't tell him, then maybe her brother, Bill Fowler, could be made to do so. It was even possible, he reasoned, that Brandon might have gone to ground at his friends' homestead. No, he decided, not likely. Too many people would know, and one or two of them might talk to strangers about what they knew.

He sprinted back to his black and swung into the saddle. Turning the horse, he rode into the sun.

Helen Simmons was collecting eggs from her chicken coop when Ki rode toward her some time later. She looked up from her work and raised one hand to shield her eyes from the sun. She gave Ki neither a greeting nor any sign of recognition. She merely stood there, her half-filled wicker basket of eggs in one hand, the other lowered to her side.

"Helen, I need your help," Ki said as he reached her and dismounted. "I need to know where Mike Brandon is."

Helen sighed and looked away from him. "I had hoped you would have given up your pursuit of Mike by now."

"I haven't. He's kidnapped Jessie again."

Helen met Ki's penetrating gaze. "A *second* time? I don't believe for one minute that Mike kidnapped your lady friend a *first* time."

"Last time I was here I didn't have any way to make you believe me, but this time I've got proof that Brandon's kidnapped Jessie." Ki dug the note Harrison had given him out of his pocket and handed it to Helen.

"What is this?"

"Read it."

She did. Then, looking up at Ki, she said, "I can't believe Mike would do a thing like this."

"Didn't your brother ever tell you that Brandon had kidnapped Jessie?"

"My brother? No, of course he didn't. What has Bill got to do with this?"

"After we three met in town and you two came home here, I trailed your brother, who led me directly to Brandon's cabin, where I found Jessie and got her safely away from them."

"You mean to tell me that Bill was mixed up in a kidnapping?"

"All I know for certain is that he knew Brandon had kidnapped Jessie, and he went to warn him that I was looking for him."

Helen lowered her eyes and then shook her head in dismay. In a low voice she said, "If my brother had anything to do with kidnapping your friend, he would go to jail, wouldn't he, as Mike will?"

"I'm not interested in putting anybody behind bars. I'm only interested in finding Jessie and taking her away from here before Brandon—or anybody else—does her any harm."

Helen looked off into the distance. She bit her lip in silence for a long moment. Then she turned back to Ki and said, "I can take you to Mike Brandon."

Ki wanted to whoop with joy. Instead, he simply said, "Thank you, Helen."

"It's not much farther," Helen said later as she drove her wagon west with Ki riding by her side. "Mike moved out of his cabin and into an abandoned soddy on the Kinkaid farm. Or what used to be the Kinkaid farm. The Kinkaids moved on when the land played out."

As Helen went on speaking about inconsequentials—the weather, the fact that one of her hens had gone broody—he knew that she was talking about mundane matters in order to avoid talking about the one thing that was probably uppermost in her mind. Thus, he was prepared for her question when it finally came.

"What are you going to do to Mike?" she asked him in a halting voice.

Kill him were the words that came to Ki's mind, but he didn't utter them. Instead, he answered, "Take Jessie away from him."

"That's all?"

Ki heard the hopeful note in Helen's voice.

"That's all—if he doesn't put up a fight."

"And if he does?"

"I'll put up a fight of my own."

They were silent after that until Helen suddenly broke the oppressive silence by saying, "That's the soddy. Straight ahead."

"Stop the wagon," Ki ordered.

"But we're still a quarter of a mile from the place," Helen protested.

"Do what I say, woman!"

When Helen had brought her horse to a halt and put on the break, she looked questioningly at Ki.

"Stay here," he told her.

"You're expecting trouble, aren't you?"

"Stay here," he repeated and dismounted. "I'll tie my horse to the back of your wagon, if you don't mind."

When Helen made no objection, he did so and then began to run lightly toward the soddy, approaching it at an angle that kept him out of the line of vision of anyone looking out the crude building's single window. When he reached his goal, he flattened his back against the sod wall and eased toward the open window. When he was next to it, he remained motionless, listening.

He could hear the voices of two men talking perfunctorily inside the soddy but not well enough to hear the words being spoken. He ducked down and went under the window, on his way to the door that hung lopsidedly on rotting leather hinges and which was flanked by two ground-hitched horses.

He thought again of a stone thrown at an egg. His body, the stone, Brandon and whoever was with him, the egg. A frontal assualt. A surprise attack. He went through the door like a shot out of a gun. His first karate chop with the edge of his outstretched hand caught Bill Fowler on the side of the neck and provoked a strangled

172

cry of pain from the man as he went down. Turning swiftly to face Brandon, who was coming for him fast, Ki raised his leg and, balancing on his other leg, delivered a violent kick to Brandon's midsection, which doubled him over.

Fowler sprang to his feet and lunged at Ki, who sidestepped the frontal attack, seized Fowler by the shoulders, and sent him hurtling into the sod wall. Before Ki could turn around again, Brandon was on him, bringing him down to the dirt floor. The two men fought each other, throwing fists furiously but neither of them managing to land any telling blows on the other. Finally Ki sprang to his feet, and then, as Brandon rose, he ducked down, seized the man with both hands, raised him high above his head, and threw him at Fowler, who was on the verge of rejoining the fray.

Fowler went down with Brandon landing on top of him.

Ki slipped a *shuriken* from his pocket. "If either of you men makes another move, this little beauty will split your skull. Now, where's Jessie?"

The two men on the floor looked up at him in amazement. Then they looked blankly at each other.

Ki repeated his question, taking a menacing step toward them as he did so.

"How the hell do we know where she is?" Brandon blurted out, his eyes on the deadly weapon in Ki's upraised hand. "You took her from us—that's the last we saw of her."

Ki's eyes narrowed. "You're lying. You kidnapped her again."

"Mister, you're loco," Fowler muttered. "Crazy as a goddam loon."

"I've got the note you sent to Harrison," Ki told Brandon. He took it from his pocket and tossed it on the floor in front of Brandon, who picked it up and read it. When he had finished doing so, he looked up at Ki. Tapping an index finger on the piece of paper, he said, "I didn't write this. That's not my signature."

173

"You're lying, Brandon. Now, if you don't tell me where you've got Jessie, I'll—"

"Don't hurt them!"

The cry had come from the doorway, where Helen Simmons stood, her hands clasped together and held in front of her chest.

"Please don't hurt them, Ki!"

He ignored her as he said, "Were you with him, Fowler, when he took Jessie out of the hotel through the kitchen? Were you and Brandon the two men who kidnapped Jessie, or did Brandon hire thugs to do that job?"

"I don't know what you're talking about!" a frightened Fowler exclaimed.

"Neither do I!" Brandon declared firmly.

But Ki had heard neither response because his mind was suddenly reeling. The last question he had spoken echoed in his thoughts: *Were you and Brandon the two men who kidnapped Jessie, or did Brandon hire thugs to do the job?*

Two men. Those two words pounded in Ki's mind. He recalled Ben Harrison using them. The board chairman had spoken them, he recalled, in the lobby of the Parker House after having displayed the note signed by Brandon. What had Harrison said? He had said, Ki now recalled, *I cannot and I will not risk the ruin of the Southern Pacific Railroad to appease criminals like the two men, whoever they were, who kidnapped Jessie.*

Harrison's reference to two men had gone unnoticed by Ki in his angry state at the time it had been made. But now its meaning came crashing down upon him with stunning force. If Harrison had known that two men had kidnapped Jessie, he had to have had a hand in the kidnapping.

Ki knew he had not told him that two men were involved. But Harrison had *known* that two men had been involved!

"You can search the house," Brandon was saying. "Jessie isn't here."

"Neither one of us kidnapped her," Fowler said. "That's the truth!"

"I know it is," Ki said solemnly.

The two men looked at each other and then back at Ki.

"You know it is?" Brandon repeated, clearly puzzled.

"I do now. I also know who really kidnapped Jessie this time."

"She really has been kidnapped?" an incredulous Brandon asked.

"Ben Harrison's behind it," Ki said, nodding. "Jessie disappeared from our hotel, and then Harrison showed up and gave me that note, which was supposedly signed by you. I think he must have written it."

"None of this make any sense to me," Brandon said as Helen left the doorway and went to stand beside her brother with her arm around his waist. "Why would the chairman of the board of the Southern Pacific kidnap one of his own board members?"

"I know it doesn't sound sensible, but, believe me, Harrison had a reason to do what I believe he's done and that reason is the fact that Jessie, when we returned to San Francisco after leaving you, went directly to Harrison and told him she thought you and the other settlers had legitimate grievances against the railroad. He refused to cooperate with her or compromise with you people, so she told him she was going to call a special meeting of the railroad's board of directors. She sent word to each of the men involved about such a meeting. In addition, she arranged to purchase additional stock in the company above and beyond what she already owns. Her goal was to own at least fifty-one percent of the outstanding shares, which would give her control of the company. Harrison said he would fight her. He said he would prevent her from changing any of the railroad's present policies. I think this—his kidnapping of Jessie—is his way of doing just that."

"But how do you know?" Fowler asked. "I mean, you come barging in here like a bull in a china shop and trounce Mike and me six ways to Sunday, and now all of a sudden you do an about-face and say that Harrison is the kidnapper, not us. I know we didn't kidnap the lady, but how do you know Harrison did? I mean, for sure?"

"I don't know for sure. But when Harrison came to me with that note, which he claimed came from Brandon, he mentioned that two men had kidnapped Jessie. I had earlier learned that fact from a chef at the Parker House. But Harrison had no way of knowing it unless he was the man who sent those two men to get Jessie. He might even have been one of them, although I doubt that. He's the kind of man who hires other people to do his dirty work for him."

"Where are you going?" Brandon asked as Ki turned and headed for the door.

"Back to San Francisco to find Jessie before it's too late."

"What do you mean, 'before it's too late'?" Fowler inquired.

Ki halted at the door and turned back to face the trio, who were watching him intently. "Harrison isn't holding Jessie for any kind of ransom, which is what you fellows were doing when you had her. You were holding her to force the railroad to meet your demands."

"At this point, I think there's something you should know," Brandon interjected. "I never intended to hurt Jessie. If our ploy failed, I intended to let her go and then go into hiding so the law wouldn't find me. In fact, that's why I left my cabin and came here. In case Jessie— or you or Harrison—sent the law looking for me. I knew you'd tell them where to find me."

"You still haven't told us what you meant when you said you had to find Miss Starbuck 'before it's too late,'" Fowler reminded Ki.

"Harrison is going to kill her," Ki told him flatly. "It says so in the note."

Helen gasped and tightened her grip on her brother. "Why would he do a terrible thing like that?"

"To get her out of his way," Ki answered. "To keep her from trying to make things easier for you folks."

Brandon swore under his breath.

Helen left her brother and approached Ki. "I want to

176

apologize to you. I should have believed you about the kidnapping when you first came here to Groveland. But Bill never told me a thing about it." She gave her brother an accusatory glance.

"I didn't want you to know what we were trying to do," Fowler explained to her. "That way, if you didn't know, nobody could consider you an accomplice of ours."

Ki turned to leave.

"Wait!" Brandon was suddenly beside him. "I'm going to San Francisco with you."

Ki studied the man closely but chose not to question his motive. "You're sure you want to do that? There could be trouble. Bad trouble. Harrison's a dangerous man."

"So can I be when someone I care about is threatened," Brandon said.

So that's it, Ki thought. He said, "You'll be a good man to have on my side. Let's go."

"Be careful," Helen said as she and Fowler followed Ki and Brandon out of the house.

"Good luck, Mike," Fowler said. "You, too, Ki."

"When is the next northbound train due, do you know?" Ki asked Brandon as they swung into their saddles and rode away together.

"Not until late this afternoon. Are we taking it?"

"No, we're not. We can't afford to wait around for it. We've got to get to Harrison as fast as we can before he can harm Jessie. If he hasn't harmed her already."

Ki said no more and neither did Brandon as both men whipped their mounts and sped toward San Francisco and whatever might await them there.

The wind whipped Ki's long black hair out behind him and dried the sweat on his face and body almost as soon as it formed. Brandon was bent low over his horse's neck as he slammed his spurs into its flanks, leaving bloody cat tracks on the otherwise smooth flesh.

Shortly after the sun had passed its meridian, Ki knew his black was not only tiring but on the verge of giving out on him. He was aware, too, that Brandon had fallen

177

behind him, and his horse's sides were heaving with the mighty effort it was making. And they still had more miles to travel than Ki wanted to think about. He decided they had to stop to rest their horses. If they didn't, he was sure they wouldn't have any horses left for the remainder of their journey.

Spotting a southbound train in the distance, Ki headed toward it, beckoning to Brandon to follow him. Both men then followed the tracks until they reached a town where Ki called a halt in front of a saloon.

"What are we stopping for?" Brandon asked him.

"I want to buy some whiskey."

"You want to buy whiskey? Now? When we've got to—"

But Ki had disappeared inside the saloon. When he emerged, he was carrying a pint bottle of bourbon. "I'll be right back," he told Brandon and then crossed the street and went inside the livery barn. He brought a gunnysack half full of oats with him when he returned.

"You got a feedbag?" he asked Brandon.

"I've got one."

"Get it."

Minutes later Ki had divided the oats into two equal portions in Brandon's feedbag and his own. He opened the bottle of bourbon and poured some of its contents into each feedbag, which he mixed by hand with the oats the bags contained. Then he hung the feedbags on the heads of both horses.

"I never saw whiskey fed to horses before," Brandon commented dubiously.

"It ought to keep them on their feet awhile longer. Long enough to get where we're going, I hope."

Once on their way again, both mounts resembled fresh horses as they galloped over level and even hilly ground. But San Francisco was still a long way away when Ki's horse began to give out on him. He slowed its pace, but that didn't help. He was in the act of drawing rein when the horse suddenly gasped noisily several times in succession, dropped its head, and fell, throwing Ki to the ground.

He got up at once and, after a brief examination of the horse, said, "It looks like I killed him."

Brandon wordlessly held out his hand. After helping Ki up behind him on his horse, they continued their journey.

It was late afternoon by the time they reached their destination. They went directly to Harrison's second-floor office and stormed past an outraged clerk who tried to prevent them from entering the board chairman's office.

"Ki!" Harrison exclaimed as they burst into the room that was filled with a number of men, only one of whom, besides Harrison himself, that Ki recognized—Chet Langley.

"What's he doing here?" Harrison bellowed from his seat behind his desk, pointing a finger at Brandon. Then, in a softer tone of voice, "You captured him, I take it. Am I correct, Ki?"

"You're incorrect. Where's Jessie, Harrison?"

Harrison gave Ki a bewildered look. "Where's Jessie?" he repeated. "How would I know? If anybody knows, *he* knows." Again he jabbed a finger in Brandon's direction.

"What's this all about, may I ask?" one of the men in the room asked. "Has this something to do with the meeting Jessie called, which we've all come here to attend, Benjamin?"

"In a way, yes, it has something to do with that. But as I was just about to explain to you gentlemen, such a meeting is unnecessary—or should I say not appropriate—at this time since Jessie Starbuck has been kidnapped by that man standing right there."

All eyes except Ki's turned to Brandon.

"He's lying to you," Ki told the assemblage. "He's right in saying that Jessie was kidnapped. But he's wrong in saying Mike Brandon kidnapped her, and he damn well knows it. Two men abducted Jessie from the Parker House last night. Harrison might have been one of them."

Harrison's jaw dropped. "That's preposterous!"

179

"Not so preposterous," Ki insisted. "I'll tell you why I know you took her or had her taken, Harrison. When you and I talked at the desk in the Parker House and you claimed Brandon had kidnapped Jessie based on that phony note you gave me, you made a reference to the fact that two men had taken her. That remark didn't register with me at the time. But it did later on. Now, how, Harrison, could you have known that two men had kidnapped Jessie unless you had been one of them or had hired them to do the deed?"

Harrison tried to speak, couldn't. He glanced nervously at Chet Langley.

"Where is she?" Ki asked again.

"I don't *know* where she is!" Harrison lied.

Ki vaulted over Harrison's desk, hauled the man up out of his chair, wrapped his left arm around his neck, and with the index finger of his free right hand began to press firmly on a spot on the back of Harrison's neck known to ninja warriors as the *Nin Chu Tsubo*. He maintained the pressure for ten seconds, ignoring the exclamations of alarm from the other men in the room, and then gradually released it.

As Langley, muttering an oath, lunged forward, Brandon seized him and twisted his arm up behind his back, preventing the man from coming to the rescue of his employer. A pocketknife appeared in Brandon's hand, and he held its blade against Langley's throat. "Don't anybody move," he ordered the assembled men. "If anybody does, this man is going to get cut."

They all remained motionless as Ki dropped Harrison's limp form into his chair. "You can't move, can you?" he asked the man, who was staring up at him with fear-filled eyes.

"*Noooo*," Harrison said in a barely audible voice.

"Now it's your limbs that cannot move," Ki said, his voice hard. "But in three days your heart will also not be able to move. It will stop."

"Somebody—help *meeee*," Harrison managed to murmur.

"I am the only one who can help you, Harrison," Ki

180

said. "I will restore you to normalcy—when you tell me where Jessie is." Ki silently prayed that Harrison would not tell him that Jessie was beyond rescue.

Harrison said nothing.

Ki turned to leave.

"*Pleeease!*"

Ki crossed the room and started to go through the door leading to the outer office.

Harrison screamed, the sound little more than a sibilant sigh.

Ki returned. "Tell me."

"She's in an empty warehouse." Harrison gave Ki its address.

"If you're lying to me—"

"Not lying."

"Is she alive?"

"I don't know—she might be."

Ki went behind Harrison and adroitly twisted the vertebrae in the man's back, allowing Harrison's strength to return to him. "Get up," he ordered. "You and Langley are coming with me. The rest of you men stay right here. I'll be back, and I'll explain everything to you."

He dragged Harrison to his feet and marched the man out of the room. Brandon, behind him, was doing the same with Langley.

They stole a four-seated surrey that was parked outside and drove wildly down the street, heading for the address Harrison had given him.

"I had to get rid of her," Harrison said plaintively from his seat next to Ki. "She would have ruined my railroad."

"If she's hurt—or worse," Ki said, "I will put you back in the state in which you were a little while ago, and I will not free you from that state. Not ever. I will leave you to die like a dog."

"Oh, Lord God in Heaven, have mercy on me!" Harrison wailed.

"You'd better keep on praying He has mercy on you," Ki muttered. "Because I won't have any at all."

"There it is," Harrison said, pointing to a building at

the base of the hill around which the ocean was beginning to flow.

Ki stopped the surrey and dragged Harrison from it. "Show me where she is!"

"The cellar," Harrison said as Brandon forced Langley out of the surrey.

The four men, two of them prisoners of the other two, hurried through the water that was making mud of the ground beneath their feet and into the warehouse.

"That way," Langley said. "Through that door over there."

Ki went through the door, and his heart almost stopped as he saw Jessie below him tied to the upright supporting the sagging ceiling, water that had seeped into the cellar covering the lower half of her body.

"Ki!" she cried.

He turned Harrison over to Brandon and then bounded down the steps into the quickly rising tide of water. Without saying a word, he began to untie the ropes that bound Jessie to the upright. One final knot defeated him. Try as he might, he could not untie it. "Brandon!" he yelled. "Give me your knife!"

Brandon tossed it down to him.

Ki caught the knife and sliced through the recalcitrant knot and then through the ropes that bound Jessie's wrists together.

He had no sooner done so than Harrison made a run for the stairs leading up from the cellar.

Langley, seeing his chance to escape, struck Brandon a blow on the side of the head, which temporarily stunned the man.

"Let's go, Jessie!" Ki yelled and, grabbing her hand, led her up the stairs. At the top of them he took a *shuriken* from his pocket and threw it at Harrison. It caught the man in the calf just as he was about to go through the outer door of the warehouse.

Harrison screamed, staggered, and went down.

Ki turned just in time to see Brandon hit Langley with a right uppercut and a left jab, both blows connecting and knocking the man backward and sending him tumbling head over heels down the stairs.

"Help her," Ki said to Brandon as Jessie's body began to sag and when Brandon had joined him and draped one of Jessie's arms around his broad shoulders, he went over to where Harrison lay weeping on the floor and clutching his injured leg with both hands. He bent down and pulled the *shuriken* free, causing Harrison to scream in pain. "Get up," he ordered. "Get back in the surrey."

"I can't walk," Harrison protested.

"You either walk or I'm going to throw you into the cellar."

"You can't! I'll drown."

Ki wiped the bloody shuriken on Harrison's coat, pocketed it, and returned to Brandon and Jessie. Together the two men helped Jessie outside. A limping Harrison joined them a few minutes later.

Then, as Ki prepared to drive away from the warehouse, Harrison said, "Langley—what happened to Langley?"

"I forgot all about him," Brandon said. "I'll go get him."

The other three waited, Jessie shivering not from cold but from shock. Ki put an arm around her. "You're going to be all right. You'll be fine."

"If it hadn't been for you—" she began.

But Ki interrupted her. "If it hadn't been for me and Mike Brandon."

She managed a small smile.

"Ki," Brandon said as he emerged alone from the warehouse and rejoined them. "Langley's dead."

Harrison gasped. "Dead?"

"He must have hit his head and knocked himself out when he fell down the stairs. He drowned."

"That is, without a doubt, the most amazing story I have ever heard in my life," cried Charles Chalmers, a member of the Southern Pacific's board of directors, when Jessie had finished giving him and the other board members gathered in Harrison's office a detailed account of

183

what had happened to her since her arrival in San Francisco.

"You were kidnapped not once but *twice*!" exclaimed another man. "My word, that is certainly extraordinary!"

"But you're quite all right now despite your recent ordeal?" prompted a concerned Chalmers.

"Oh, yes," Jessie replied. "A little the worse for wear, but I'm fine really." Then, after glancing in Mike Brandon's direction, she said, "Now, about the items I mentioned that I thought we should reconsider. . . ."

"I think you've made a most impressive case, you and Mr. Brandon, for lowering the line's terminal rate," a board member declared. "We won't go bankrupt if we give the settler's a fair break, which I now realize we should have been doing all along, as Jessie has just so successfully argued."

"And we will gain their goodwill," Jessie pointed out, and this time when she glanced at Brandon, he was grinning from ear to ear.

"I, for one, will cast my vote on Jessie's side in the matter of the evictions," Chalmers announced. "Mr. McCabe, what say you?"

"I, too, think we should sell that land to the settlers at the original price we proposed to them—two-fifty to five dollars an acre," McCabe stated. "Now, don't get me wrong, gentlemen. I'm not going soft in the head in my old age. I'm still a good businessman, I'll have you know, and I believe such a move will benefit the railroad in the long run. We know the settlers are industrious and productive people. If we can keep such people on that land, we are assuring ourselves of heavy freight and passenger traffic. In short, the Southern Pacific will make money."

As the discussion continued, only two board members objected to Jessie's proposals. Then a vote was taken, its outcome preordained. The majority voted in favor of lowering the terminal rate at once and selling the railroad's land to the settlers at the original offering price.

"I thank you, gentlemen, for responding so promptly

to my request for a board meeting," Jessie told them. "I am delighted at the outcome of the voting. I'm sure the line we all care about will be stronger for the actions we have taken here today."

As the men began to say their good-byes to one another and to Jessie, she turned to Ki and whispered, "You and Mike deserve the credit for all this. If the two of you hadn't saved my life, none of this would have happened, and Ben Harrison would be well on his way, in my opinion, to ruining the railroad."

"As it is, he'll be spending a good number of years in jail on a charge of kidnapping and attempted murder."

"Did you see the shocked look on his face when we turned him over to the police on our way here?" Brandon asked as he joined them. "I don't think he believed what was happening to him."

"Neither will Jim Bisbee when the police catch up with him for his part in kidnapping me," Jessie said.

"I'm glad they don't catch up with all criminals, though," Ki said.

Jessie frowned. "Whatever do you mean by that remark?"

"If they had caught up with us for stealing that surrey that was parked outside before we were able to return it with its owner being none the wiser, we might be sharing Ben Harrison's jail cell."

Jessie laughed and then, turning to Brandon, said, "I suppose you'll be wanting to hurry back to Fresno County to give your friends the good news about what was done here today."

"Oh, I'm not in all that much of a hurry," Brandon said.

Ki noticed the looks of longing that passed between Jessie and Brandon. "Mike," he said, "here's fifty dollars. When you get back to your old stomping ground, I'd be obliged to you if you'd give this money to the farrier in Groveland to pay for the horse and gear I rented from him."

"I'll be glad to do that, Ki."

"Jessie, if you and Mike will excuse me, I have some things I want to take care of."

"You're excused," Jessie said and gave Ki a hug. "Thanks for being so discreet."

When Ki and the board members had all left Harrison's office, Brandon offered Jessie his arm. She took it, and together they also left the office, both of them knowing they were on their way to Jessie's room in the Parker House, and both of them also knowing exactly what they were going to do when they got there.

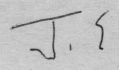

Watch for

LONE STAR AND THE DEVIL WORSHIPERS

96th novel in the exciting LONE STAR series
from Jove

Coming in August!